Cover design by Miblart



Published by Higher Bank Books

# RESIST THE DARKNESS

A Post Apocalyptic EMP Survival Thriller

RYAN CASEY

## GET A POST APOCALYPTIC NOVEL FOR FREE

To instantly receive an exclusive post apocalyptic novel totally free, sign up for Ryan Casey's author newsletter at: ryancaseybooks.com/fanclub

# CHAPTER ONE

***Two months after the blackout...***

Christopher Parker always prided himself on his ability to keep his emotions in check.

But seeing his mother dying before his eyes really changed everything he thought he believed on that front.

It was dark. The only light in this room came from the flickering candles, which kept going out in the draught. There was always a bad draught in this house. Ever since he was a kid. He remembered sitting in front of the television, wrapping himself in a blanket and watching whatever Friday night movie Mum picked up from the Blockbuster video store just down the road. Mum telling him to get an extra blanket if he was cold.

And he felt so bad, looking back. He hadn't realised at the time just how much Mum was struggling financially. Just how momentous an endeavour something as seemingly simple as turning the central heating on actually was.

And it didn't help that he had five brothers. A big family. So many mouths to feed. Sometimes didn't get fed at all.

No wonder he'd appreciated his food so much in the years that followed.

But Friday night video rental night was always a thing. He and his five siblings all huddled up together. Mum on the sofa behind them. Teeth chattering. Blueish complexion to her.

He looked down at her lying on the sofa right now, and he found himself right back there, all over again.

She stared back up at him with those bright blue eyes. Her face was gaunt. She was always a big woman. Still had some weight to her, even though their starvation had reached new levels over the last two months. Christopher found it impossible to believe. So hard to understand, as he looked down at her pale, sweaty skin. At those watery eyes, so bloodshot and red, unblinking.

Holding on to that cold hand, which squeezed him so tightly, still so strong, still so weighty despite everything.

"Hold on, Mum," Christopher whispered. Stroking her damp hair off her forehead, most of it just falling away. "You hold on—"

She coughed. Spluttered blood and phlegm right into his face. He felt a hint of disgust as he tasted the metallic tang on his lips. He wasn't good with blood. Never good around blood.

But at the same time... he knew he needed to be as rational and as composed as he'd been throughout his entire life. Seeing emotions as just emotions. Seeing thoughts as just thoughts.

And sometimes, seeing the difficult decisions as the only decisions that could be made.

He heard footsteps creaking outside the room, and his stomach sank. Glynn, his oldest brother. And then there was Peter, too. The only two surviving brothers. The only ones left.

And yet they were out there while he was in here with Mum at what had to be the end.

She'd fallen ill two weeks ago. Well, she was in her seventies, and she'd been ill for a while. The blackout hadn't helped. Especially when she wasn't getting her usual heart medication.

But recently, she'd really deteriorated. Caught a nasty bug. COVID, probably. It only stood to reason that something like that would make a resurgence in a world so badly sanitised. Not to mention a whole crop of new diseases surfacing. The streets literally reeked of raw sewage at this point; it wasn't even shocking anymore.

He didn't know what Mum's illness was. Not for definite. He couldn't know. Truth was, it didn't matter. She was sick. Really sick. Wheezing away. Vomiting a lot. The air reeked of bile and shit and piss.

And she was only getting worse by the day.

He wanted to go out to his brothers. Wanted to ask them what to do next. Because as much as he was the rational one, he was never the decision-maker. It was never a position he was comfortable in.

But Mum wouldn't let go of his hand as he stood there in this darkness, the March winds battering the house outside. The whole place creaking. So cold.

Little Gingey, Mum's cat, watching with her big eyes from the corner of the room.

Looking at Christopher nervously. Never had liked him, that cat. Christopher wasn't sure why. He always liked animals.

Maybe it was his breath.

Some people commented on his breath being bad. Maybe cats judged him for that, too.

He felt Mum's hand squeeze tighter. Turned around, waited for her to mumble whatever other nonsensical words she had left. Waited for her to gasp with that shrivelled up mouth.

But there was something different about Mum when she looked up at him this time.

She was nudging her head back, just a little.

Like she was gesturing him to come closer.

He moved his head towards her. Closer to her face. To her vomit breath.

And then she leaned into his ear. He could feel the faint warmth of her breath on his skin. Hear her teeth chattering lightly.

She whispered the words to him that sent shivers up his spine.

He stepped away from her. Let go of her hand.

Looked down at her as she lay there.

And he ran over what she'd said to him, again and again and again.

And as much as the rational part of his brain screamed at him that it was right, that it made sense, especially with how starving he was, with how scarce resources were... the emotional side of him couldn't be here.

It couldn't listen to it.

Couldn't hear it.

Mum lay there. Staring up at Christopher. Coughing again, now.

And Christopher knew after hearing those words that he couldn't be in this room anymore.

He had to get away.

He had to escape.

He couldn't be in here.

And he couldn't accept the fact that it was because the thought had been planted in his head.

The thought he didn't want to think about.

The thought he didn't want to entertain.

But the thought he couldn't push away.

He stepped out of the lounge. Closed the door.

Didn't glance around. Not once. Because he couldn't look her in the eyes. Not after what she'd said. Not again.

Peter and Glynn both stood there. Two opposites. Glynn short, fat, and balding. Peter unnaturally tall and skinny.

"Well?" Glynn said.

Christopher looked at them both, and as much as he wanted

to fight for his mum, as much as he wanted to save her, he knew it was time.

"I think... I think it's time we did the kindest thing for her."

Glynn's eyes widened.

Peter lowered his head.

Both of them got it. Both of them understood.

It was Christopher who had been postponing the inevitable all this time, after all.

Trying to prolong things. For his own selfish reasons, maybe.

Glynn reached over to him. Put a hand on his shoulder.

"We're doing the right thing, Chris."

And then he walked past him.

Opened the door.

Christopher didn't want to turn around. He didn't want to look.

But he had to.

He looked around.

Saw his mum lying there on the sofa.

Glynn walking over to her.

Peter walking past and into the room.

He stopped at the door.

Stopped as Glynn stroked Mum's hair.

As he reached for a pillow.

As she looked back over at Christopher, only Christopher.

He knew he was her favourite, and he knew he was betraying her.

Peter closed the door.

He heard some shuffling. Some struggling.

And then nothing.

He waited. Waited by the door. Heart racing. Knowing full well what was coming but not wanting to accept it. Not wanting to face up to it.

But then the door opened, and he knew from the looks on his brothers' faces that it was done.

They hugged. All three of them hugged. They cried, while behind them, the lifeless mound on the sofa where Mum lay stared back at him.

And as Christopher stood there crying, staring into that dark, candlelit room, he couldn't hide away from the last words Mum said to him.

He couldn't help letting the rational side of his brain creep in, amidst all the emotion, as his starving stomach called out...

*"You have to, Christopher. You have to. Just like we spoke of. It's my last wish. For you. For all of you. You know it's the right thing to do..."*

# CHAPTER TWO

***Four months later...***

Aoife felt the thoughts and the memories simmering to the surface, and she knew there was only one thing she could do to help.

It was morning. Light peeked in through the cracks in the curtains. The living room was stuffy, clammy. A stench of sweat and a bitter hint of vomit in the air. It reminded Aoife of when she went through a bout of depression and anxiety in her late teens. The months she'd spent just confined to her bedroom. That clamminess in the room; that warmth in the air, suffocating.

And just the memory of how horrible she'd felt in those years made her feel even worse right now. Brought the memories all crashing back.

But they weren't the memories she was trying to suppress.

The memories she was trying to suppress were so much more terrifying. So much more haunting. So much worse.

She stood in the middle of the lounge in this place she called home and stared at the bottle of gin in her hands. Edinburgh Gin. Raspberry flavour. Never used to really like gin before the power went out. Always found it hard to enjoy. Much preferred a beer or a nice crisp lager.

But right now, she'd actually developed quite a taste for gin. Well. That wasn't entirely accurate. She'd developed quite a taste for *all* alcohol over the last six months.

Not the healthiest habit to pick up in her early thirties, sure.

But fuck. What did it matter anymore anyway?

The world had gone to shit. And it wasn't getting fixed any time soon.

Drink was about the only effective way to pass the time before the end inevitably arrived.

Because it was coming for everyone.

And besides, it kept the thoughts away.

The memories away.

She saw the sunlight peeking through the dirty window. Somewhere out there, she heard a child laughing on the streets of the estate she'd called home for the last half a year. And it made her smile. For just a moment, it filled her with optimism. Filled her with hope.

Because it was the sound of normality. The sound of happiness. The sound of innocence, before the world was robbed of all of it.

But then, following that laugh, she heard a cough. A nasty gasping cough. And it snapped her right back into the moment.

There were a lot of sick people on the estate. It looked like some sort of respiratory infection had run rife. Probably COVID.

And in a world without sanitation, in a world where vaccinations had worn off, and antibodies were waning, in a world where groups were tightly pressed together in close quarters, it just stood to reason that disease would take hold.

She heard the coughing outside. She knew there'd be another death today. There were around forty people in this community now, but at its height, there were eighty—and that wasn't even that long ago. Most of the elderly were dead, after bravely surviving the first wave of the blackout.

And the hardest thing to swallow was that supplies were running so low that weirdly, a reduction in the number of mouths needed to feed was probably logistically a good thing.

And that's what made Aoife shake her head. That's what made her open the lid of the bottle.

Because she could barely face living in a world where these kinds of compromises had to be considered.

Where death had to be seen as something of a... a bonus?

No. It just felt wrong.

She pulled the bottle to her lips, and suddenly a flash of a memory came to mind.

That day six months ago, in the thick of winter.

Nathan.

Moira.

James killing them both.

Max falling to the road, and...

She closed her eyes. Shook her head.

Poured the gin into her mouth, neat.

Felt it burning against her tongue, against her lips. And even though it was objectively an unpleasant sensation, she felt like she was growing used to it. Getting accustomed to it.

To the point that she knew if she had to resort to mouthwash to get her kick, she could probably just about handle it.

She swigged it back. Gulp after gulp.

But the more she swigged it, the more the memories came.

And the more vivid and disturbing they were.

Her brother, Seth, kneeling before her.

Holding the gun to his head and killing him.

Harold shooting the kid, Sam, up at the cottages in the woods.

Max.

Max and Rex and...

She drank more of the drink. More and more. And before she knew it, in no time at all, the lounge was spinning around her. She could barely sit, let alone stand.

But then the bottle was empty, and she needed something —anything.

She got up. Walked across the lounge, over towards the kitchen. The kitchen of this place she was told to call home, but felt so empty, so void of life, so void of everything...

She reached the cupboard where she kept the booze when she saw something she couldn't quite believe.

There were no bottles in there.

It was empty.

She stared in there, head spinning. Not sure how much longer she could stay on her feet. The fear invaded her.

Fear of what would happen to her if she didn't keep drinking.

Fear of the memories.

Fear of—

She saw the graves in her mind.

Nathan.

Moira...

And she thought of Max.

Of standing over him, giving him CPR, trying to bring him back.

She saw Harry, who she'd left behind in the bus, only to survive before getting beaten to a pulp trying to save her.

Then the girl who'd died when she'd been fleeing the falling plane.

And Max...

*"Please, Max. Don't leave me. Please..."*

She saw the vision of him lying dead on the road flash through her mind.

Saw the lifelessness in his eyes.

Felt the guilt all over again.

Then she saw the old bottle of bleach at the back of the cupboard.

Without even thinking, without any control over her body, she reached in there.

She opened the lid.

Smelled the strong, biting stench of the fluid.

Stared down at it. Hands shaking.

"I'm sorry," she said. "I'm so sorry."

She went to pour it down her throat when her front door opened.

She looked around and saw someone standing there.

A man standing there.

Tall.

Bearded.

Not smiling—never smiling—but those kind, friendly eyes peering over at her.

Standing there and then running over to her.

"It's okay," he said. Taking the bleach bottle from her hand. Putting it on the side. Helping her to her feet as she sobbed and cried and holding her. "It's okay, Aoife. It's okay. It's Max. It's me. It's okay. Everything's gonna be okay."

# CHAPTER THREE

"Come on. Get this down you. It'll do you good."

Aoife stared at the steaming bowl of murky brown broth before her and she was pretty certain if she put it anywhere near her mouth, she'd throw the whole thing up everywhere.

"I'm not sure I'm really in the mood for... whatever this is."

Max shook his head and sighed as he sat beside her on her sofa. He'd wrapped a blanket over her. Helped her off the kitchen floor, onto the sofa. Made sure she got plenty of water down her. She'd no idea how long had passed since the meltdown this morning, but it looked like it was afternoon now.

And Max hadn't left her side. Not once.

Rex sat in the corner of her lounge, wagging his tail reluctantly. Staring over at Aoife like he didn't even recognise her anymore. And that made her feel sad. Guilty. She was the one who'd rescued him from hell on the first day of the blackout, after all. She was the one who'd sworn to protect him.

But now Max looked after him because... well. It was no secret that he could do a better job of looking after him than Aoife could. Being with a pisshead wasn't exactly great for any animal's health when you really thought about it.

And... well. Aoife wasn't convinced having Rex around was particularly good for her, either.

Because he wasn't exactly a young dog. And if anything happened to him...

She just wasn't sure she could lose anyone else.

She certainly couldn't let anyone else in.

"Go on," Max said. "Just a sip. It's nice. Squirrel bone soup."

Aoife almost vomited in her mouth. "Really selling it to me."

"It'll get your energy levels up. Go on. Remember what you were like to me six months ago, back in my place. Forcing me to eat that fucking awful porridge."

"At least it didn't have squirrel bones in it."

Max smirked a little. Like he was enjoying this.

But she could see the concern in his eyes.

She shrugged, shook her head, took a sip. If only to please him. It wasn't pleasant. Then again, no food or liquid was pleasant right now. Not with a sore throat and a banging head like she had.

But it was actually not so bad in the end. And she had to concede she felt a little better already.

"Better?" Max asked.

Aoife sighed. "Sort of."

"Told you it'd do the trick. Better than bloody bleach, anyway."

Aoife looked up at him, felt her cheeks flushing. She couldn't explain that momentary temptation to drink the bleach. She knew the pain it would cause. She knew it would inevitably kill her.

But the scariest thing?

It felt like the most natural thing to do before Max came wandering in out of nowhere.

The right thing to do.

"We don't have to talk about it," Max said.

And she appreciated that. She couldn't remember exactly what prompted her. Didn't know what made her do anything these days. Only she'd had visions of those she'd lost. Those she'd felt responsible for losing. The people she'd bonded with in some small way or large way...

And then Max.

The memory of him lying on the road.

Thinking she'd lost him.

Trying to give him CPR, trying to save him, thinking he was gone.

Only for a miracle to happen.

Springing back to life when she'd given up on him.

They gathered medical supplies from one of the nearby centres. They pumped all they could into his bloodstream, and they helped him. Saved him.

The estate that almost cost them both their lives ended up their salvation.

And it was a good place. For a while, people put what happened in the early days behind them. Pulled together for the greater good, ready to ride out this blackout, however long it lasted.

Only nobody really thought the blackout would last as long as it had. The blackout dragged out of winter and into spring, now into summer.

And at different paces, people realised that this wasn't something that was going to be fixed.

This was the new normal.

And that was quite a bitter pill to swallow.

"Feel a bit better?"

Aoife nodded. "You can go now."

"I'm not going anywhere," Max said. "You know, you should speak with Sam. Former priest. Never been a religious guy myself, but he's a good bloke to offload to—"

"I'm fine. Really. You should go. Sure you've got patients to see to."

Max opened his mouth like he was going to say something. And she felt bad for snapping at him. She wanted to let him be close to her. She felt safe when he was close. The only person she felt comfortable letting this close at all.

But that also scared her.

Terrified her.

"I made you something, anyway," he said.

Aoife frowned. "Made me something?"

"It's... it's just a little something." He reached into his pocket. Pulled out this weird chunk of wood. Held it out to her.

"It's... a piece of wood," she said. "Wow. Thanks."

"It's a boat."

Aoife smirked. "A boat? I don't see a boat."

"It's a boat, alright? Mick taught us about crafting things out of wood. A bit pointless, I know. But something to occupy the mind. And the people there are alright. I... I wanted to make it for you."

Aoife held it in her palm. Smiled at Max. It was terrible. Definitely not a boat. But she appreciated the gesture, she supposed.

"Thanks," she said.

Max nodded. Blushing a little. And then he stood up. Wiped his black T-shirt in the way he always did. "You know... you should come down some day. It'll be good for you."

Aoife's hairs on the back of her neck stood on end. "I'm fine. Really."

"It might be good to get out of the house—"

"Since when have you become the authority on making connections with people?" Aoife said.

Max looked at her a little more sternly now. "Since I realised sitting around and beating myself up about things I can't change doesn't do shit. Since I realised a life in fear of making connections isn't a life worth living."

He stared at her. She stared back at him. She wanted to say so much more to him. She wanted to scream at him about how hard this was for her. How impossible it was.

But then she just shook her head.

Turned away.

"You know the way out."

"You sure you're going to be—"

"I'm fine."

She stared at the corner of the room. Heard Max sigh, shuffle around a few times.

Then eventually, he walked away.

She heard Rex follow him. She wanted to reach down and pat him as he passed by.

But that thought of connection pained her.

That thought of what she could lose pained her.

She heard the front door open.

Felt the summer breeze creep inside.

"There's things you could offer this community, Aoife. You're strong. You're intelligent. You'd be excellent at hunting and training others how to hunt. There's another option to being holed up in here and—"

"Bye, Max."

A pause. A pause that Aoife feared Max might fill at any second.

Then: "Bye, Aoife."

She nodded.

Waited a few more seconds.

The door closed.

The silence filled the room.

She held that wooden boat in her hand.

And an unshakable wave of sadness crashed against her.

"Don't go," she whispered to herself under her breath. "Don't... don't go."

# CHAPTER FOUR

Max walked out onto the main street of the estate, Rex by his side, and he couldn't help feeling bad about Aoife and the state she was in.

It was another damned warm afternoon. Too damned warm, in his opinion. Sure, he wasn't one to complain about the weather. Could be worse. Could be the middle of goddamned winter. They'd been lucky last winter, really. Never got as cold as it could've done.

Which was a relief. One cold winter would surely be enough to bring what remained of this community—what remained of humanity, as far as he could see it—to its knees.

He looked around at the street. Normal street to the naked eye, really. Lots of terraced houses, pretty small. A few smashed windows here and there, some of which were boarded up. But mostly okay. At the end of the street, some bags of sand stacked on top of one another and some old metal railing to mark the gates, around twenty feet high. A couple of people standing guard up some ladders up there. Not exactly the most fortified place. But it was something. Created the illusion of community. The illusion of home.

He looked beyond those markers, and a chill crept up his spine, especially seeing the trees in the distance, the hills. His old home was so close to here. So close that he could be up that hill and there in no time at all.

But he'd not been back for a long time. Only once since the estate people brought him back to life, in fact, and that was to bring what supplies he had down here.

He had no reason to go back there. It was a part of his past. A past he'd moved forward from. A past he couldn't stay bogged down in.

A past that in the last few years wasn't so happy.

Because he'd pushed everyone away. Isolated himself.

And as much as it felt like the right thing to do at the time... he saw now that living that way wasn't living at all.

Living in fear of loss was not living at all.

You couldn't avoid connection just to avoid the pain of loss. Because Max's most beautiful memories were of the moments in life he'd loved. And he wouldn't change those moments for anything. He'd go through the pain all over again if it meant not losing those memories.

It'd taken him a long-damned time to get there, but he'd got there.

But now, he saw Aoife, and he saw how deep into the hole she was in. The hole he'd gone down before. The hole that seemed impossible to drag yourself out of.

He wanted to get on with his own life.

But he couldn't just leave her to fall down the path she was going down.

Yet, at the same time... what was he supposed to do about it?

He looked around and saw a woman, Shel, coughing away in the streets. Spluttering everywhere. Looked like she was coughing up blood.

He knew he had to keep his distance. He could only encourage her to stay home, which was so frigging hard to do when he was acting as one of the doctors here. But that's all they could do now. 'Cause six months on, they didn't have the things they'd used to save his life to save other people.

Disease was running rampant. And it was only getting worse by the day.

He wanted to go over to Shel and tell her to get home. To stay home.

But at the same time, seeing her wade through the streets, stumbling side to side... he got the feeling she wouldn't even make it home.

Another one gone.

Another loss.

And the harsh reality that it was better to keep his distance. Staying alive for the rest of the community was the best service he could offer. And Shel looked way beyond saving, God bless her.

He looked down at Rex. Rex was looking thinner these days, too. Not unhealthily so. They were all feeling the poverty, after all.

But he saw the way Rex looked back at Aoife's place, head slightly lowered, tail down, and he felt sadness again. 'Cause as much as he and Rex had a bond... Aoife had given Rex to him because she thought he'd look after him better. She'd pushed Rex onto him, and as much as he agreed she wasn't in the best place and had been going down a dark path lately... there was still that bond between Rex and her that was unshakable.

And seeing Rex looking so glum, it really hit Max.

Max looked up at Aoife's place. Looked at the lounge window. He wanted her to open the curtains. To wave back at him to go back there.

He wanted to look after her.

Get her back to full strength.

He wanted to comfort her.

Because there was something about her.

A warmth he felt about her.

A warmth he'd only ever felt about one other woman in his entire life.

Kathryn.

He thought of Kathryn and David. Thought of that room they'd stood in when he'd been at death's door. Thought about how he'd gone in there. The joy he'd felt with them.

But then he remembered, as he lay dying on the road, realising that they were just thoughts. They were just memories.

And they would want nothing more than for him to honour what happened to them by living a happy life.

So he turned around.

He turned around, and he saw Aoife in that other door.

Aoife in the door of life.

He fought through the tar-like substance dragging him down to the abyss, dragged himself through that door towards Aoife, and he woke up.

He woke up, and ever since, he'd spent the time recovering. Then trying to keep this estate afloat. Teaching people how to hunt. Scavenging. Fishing. Surviving.

But things were getting more difficult than ever now. Even the natural resources seemed to be dwindling.

And it was fast becoming clear that a place like this wasn't going to be sustainable for much longer.

He looked back at Aoife's window. He wanted to go back there. To tell her how he felt. To tell her the most dangerous confession of all.

But then he lowered his head, and he sighed.

"Come on, lad," he said to Rex. "Let's go get you fed."

He turned around and walked away from Aoife's.

He swore he saw her curtain twitch.

## CHAPTER FIVE

Vincent tumbled to the road, smacked his face against the concrete, and tasted blood.

And even in this moment of pain, his prevailing thought was one of relief.

Relief that he could still feel at all.

Relief that he was still *alive* at all.

Because he'd seen what he was running from. And he had to keep on going. He had to get away.

He couldn't stay there a moment longer.

It was boiling. So warm. He was covered in sweat, and he couldn't remember the last time he wasn't absolutely drenched. His white T-shirt was ripped and torn. He had sores all over his legs, blisters all over his feet. He could barely walk anymore. His journey had been so long and taken him so far.

And yet he had to keep going. He had to keep walking.

Because if he didn't, then he knew what would happen.

He knew *exactly* what would happen.

He lifted his shaking head a little. Saw a tooth on the road amidst blood. His tooth and his blood. He smirked a little, shook his head, spat the blood from his throat. He'd keep it if there were any medical way he could get it shoved back in his gum.

But then, what was the point anymore?

What was the point in keeping it in a world where nobody would be able to fix him?

Where nobody would be able to treat him?

He grabbed it anyway and shoved it in his back pocket. Then he pushed himself back to his shaking, sore feet.

"Keep on going anyway," he muttered. "All I can do."

He heard something over his shoulder. Something that sounded like footsteps. Like voices.

He turned around. Looked back at the little suburban centre. Looked at the old betting shop, completely boarded up. Looked at the bus shelter, glass smashed out of its windows. He looked at the pigeons wandering through the street, and the rats, bigger and tamer than ever now. Confident. It was their world now. The world of the rodents.

But it was beyond there he looked.

Where he'd come from.

His heart began to race. Because he couldn't stop thinking about what was back there. Of *who* was back there, rather. He'd had so much hope. So much positivity. So much optimism.

And then, all of a sudden, it'd been snatched from him.

Snatched from him in a way he couldn't even understand.

Still couldn't comprehend.

He looked down at the marks around his wrists. The deep cuts from the binds around them. And then he smelled the burning. He tasted the blood...

He saw and smelled and tasted all these memories and saw all the visions and heard all the muffled cries and screams and—

No.

He was out now.

He was away from that now.

He turned around and walked. He knew he was probably imagining things. Probably hearing things. They weren't really here, no chance. They wouldn't come after him. After all, why would they? He was just one person. And what sort of a threat was he to them, really?

Unless...

They might think he knew too much.

They might think he could be dangerous.

He might be able to destroy the lie they told about themselves.

He felt a rare cool breeze amidst the heat. Looked back once again.

Swore he saw movement in the shadows. Coming his way.

Vincent turned again. And as sore as he was, as much as the blisters on his feet were swollen and painful, he ran. Ran as quickly as he could. Ran even though his knees were weak. Even though his back ached like mad. Even though he was tired and dehydrated, and—

A searing pain, right up his foot.

A bursting blister.

He limped over. Let out a little cry. His heart raced. His teeth chattered.

"Shit," he said, removing his torn trainer and his muddy sock. "Fuck..."

The bottom of his foot was in a bad way. Leaking pus and blood, and something green too, by the looks of things.

Infection. Some kind of infection.

He closed his eyes. Took deep breaths in through his nostrils, let them out through his mouth. *Give me a break here. Just give me a bit of luck here, for once in my damned life.*

He went to take another breath when he heard something.

This time, he was sure of it.

Someone behind him.

Someone close.

He looked back there, and his stomach turned. The hairs on the back of his neck stood on end.

In the distance, he could see someone.

He turned around again, and he ran. Didn't care about the pain in his foot, searing and intense as it was. Didn't care about any of it.

Just ran. Fast as he goddamned could.

He kept on going until that sharp pain in his foot stopped him in his tracks.

Until he was forced to stop because he couldn't go any further.

He had to go into one of the buildings around him.

He had to get away.

He had to hide.

He looked back.

Saw that figure even closer now.

Closing in on him, like in a nightmare.

Walking. That's all. Just walking towards him. Slowly. Calmly.

He gasped, and he turned, and he went to run when he saw something up ahead.

First, the people.

The people in the distance.

Behind these erected walls.

A community.

A home.

An old housing estate.

Some kind of... group?

He saw them, and he felt a combination of feelings.

First, excitement.

He could get there. He could get help. He could get away from those chasing him. He was going to be okay.

And then the next thing he felt was dread.

Total dread.

Not just for himself.

But for the people in that community.

He turned around and saw him standing right there, behind him.

His eyes were sullen and wide. He stared right at Vincent with sympathy. Like he was an animal that needed to be put down.

"You shouldn't have run, Vincent," he said. And then he glanced past him, over at the community. His eyes lighting up. "But it's a good job you did. I guess it's worked out in the long run, right?"

Vincent opened his mouth. Wanted to say something. Wanted to speak.

And then the man stepped forward.

Covered his mouth with a cloth.

A cloth that instantly made him feel tired and weak, and...

The man looked into his eyes.

"You won't feel any pain. I'll make sure of that. I promise you. I'm sorry you had to..."

He fell to the ground.

Darkness.

The next thought that crossed his mind was that the man was a liar.

A goddamned liar.

Because when he stared into the darkness and the knife buried deep into his throat, he'd never felt pain or fear like it.

# CHAPTER SIX

Aoife walked off into the woods and tried to empty her mind of all thoughts, all feelings, everything.

It was early evening. The sun was setting. She wanted to get out of the house and get walking. Max was right this morning. She'd put herself into a dangerous situation, getting so drunk and then going to drink the bleach. And she'd felt hungover and vulnerable as hell all day.

She didn't want to be at home. Not at the moment.

So she'd sneaked past the main gates and gone out into the surrounding woodlands.

It wasn't forbidden to leave the estate, per se. There was a pretty open-door policy. But generally, it was seen as better to stay put unless you were hunting, scouting. The community needed all the people and all the help it could get, and nobody wanted to risk losing any more people.

But right now, Aoife was in pretty close territory. Not so far away from the community.

And yet, as she looked back, over at the estate, through the trees, she wondered if it might be better for everybody if she just walked away. Just vanished into the night.

Better for her, certainly. That way, she could avoid any awkward goodbyes.

And surely better for the likes of Max, too. He'd understand.

She looked back and tasted vomit in her mouth. She wasn't sure where she was going, what direction she was going in. Whether she was even going to go back at all. Maybe she'd spend some time out here in the woods. Sleep out here in nature. Or maybe she'd just never go home at all.

She didn't know what she wanted. Only that she felt better here. More peaceful here.

She looked at the trees around her. Saw the squirrels running along up the branch of one of the trees. And she smiled. Always reminded her of being with Dad when she was a kid, being in nature. The things he'd taught her about the wild. About how to respect her surroundings. Show care. Show love.

She thought back to the community, and she felt guilty. Because so many people were struggling back there. Food supplies were lower now. Far scarcer. And people didn't really know how to survive there. Not properly. Well. They knew enough to get by. Or at least a few people knew enough to get by. But the vast majority there were surviving on the knowledge of others.

There was so much more she could do for the people there. So much more she knew. So many ways she could help.

And she was just letting her knowledge go to waste.

Because she was afraid.

She turned around away from the estate when she saw movement up ahead.

At first, she thought it was another animal. A deer. Or something bigger, like a dog.

And then the hairs on her arms stood on end.

Because the closer she looked, the more convinced she became that there was somebody out there in the trees.

Watching.

She stood still. Totally still. Heart racing a little faster. Sickening feeling of dread cramping her stomach right up.

There was someone there.

There was someone watching her.

There was—

And then the movement behind the thick trees shifted, and they disappeared from view.

Aoife stood still. Very still. Heart beating faster than ever. She didn't know what to do. Where to go. Or what this even meant.

She just had an eerie feeling about all of this.

"Hello?" she said.

Her voice echoed through the silence of the woods. She suddenly felt both very alone, very vulnerable, and yet very *watched* at the same time.

She kept very still. Shaking. Unable to move.

But that movement ahead of her was gone. No doubt about that.

She felt torn. Torn between turning around and heading back towards the estate.

Or investigating the movement.

And knowing what a stubborn bitch she was... she knew already what her instincts were drawing her towards.

She stepped towards the source of the movement.

Clenched her fists.

Tightened her jaw.

Heart racing so fast and heavy it was vibrating in her skull.

She shivered. Her long nails dug into her palms. She had no idea why she was heading towards the source of the movement. Curiosity, mostly.

Someone was out here, and that meant someone was watching her.

Who were they?

What did they want?

She gritted her teeth harder, and then she stepped around the part of the trees that were just about blocking her full view of the movement.

There was nobody there.

Not a sign.

Not even any trace of footprints.

She shook her head as she stood there in the breeze. Somewhere above, a crow cawed. Maybe she was imagining things. Wouldn't be the first time. Especially not after drink.

That was it. Probably *thought* she'd seen someone, when in fact, it was just an animal. Or maybe even nothing at all.

She was being ridiculous. She had to head back to the community. There was nothing for her out here.

There was...

She went to turn around when she stopped.

She saw it.

Something on the ground before her.

Footprints. Clear footprints.

She saw the footprints extending right ahead like a dot to dot unveiling itself.

Beyond the trees.

And there, she swore she saw that movement again.

Her heart beat faster now. Because she knew for definite, now. Someone had been here.

No. Someone was *still* here.

And yet, she still wanted to follow those footprints.

She still wanted to know.

She walked down alongside the prints, over towards those trees.

Over towards the path the prints led to.

She reached a thicker clump of trees, and she stopped dead.

She stood there. Heart racing. Chest tight. Fists clenched.

No turning back now.

"Come on," she said. "Just a look. That's all you have to do. Just one look."

She took a deep breath.

Then, silently as possible, she stepped around the branches.

It took her a few seconds to really focus. To really register what she was looking at.

But when she saw it, when her eyes settled, her stomach dropped.

This was serious.

# CHAPTER SEVEN

Aoife looked at the scene before her and tried to comprehend exactly what she was seeing.

The evening sun sat on the horizon, a deep red. All around, she could hear the roar of the wind against the trees. The sound of flies buzzing around beneath her.

And the smell of death.

On the ground before her, she saw a body. It was a man. He was stripped and looked like he'd been badly beaten. He was in his forties by the looks of things, a little older than Aoife. He was bound at the ankles and wrists with barbed wire.

Around his face and neck, a pool of deep red blood.

Aoife's body turned completely cold. Looking down at this body, a sense of urgency slipped in. Urgency to get away from here. Urgency to get back to the estate.

Because it was quite clear. This man had been murdered. He had been killed.

Which meant there was someone dangerous out there.

Someone dangerous, right on the doorstep of the estate.

She went to turn around and run back towards the estate when she saw movement over to the right.

She froze.

Totally solid.

The movement she'd seen just before. Movement she'd almost forgotten about in the drama of finding the body.

It was here again.

She saw the figure moving between the trees. Slow at first. Then quickly. Then not moving at all.

And as she stood there, frozen solid, hands icy, she realised how vulnerable she felt. Just how much like *prey* she felt.

Because this guy. She didn't know who he was, where he'd come from, or what he'd done to deserve this.

But he looked like he'd been through hell before he'd died.

She stayed totally still. Like standing still was actually going to do her any good here.

And then she realised that if there were someone watching her, staying still would be no good. It might be shock, but she knew there was only one thing she could actually do.

She had to get away from here.

She had to run.

She went to run when she saw the movement again.

She stepped back. Stood behind a tree. Heart racing. Sweat trickling down her face.

She heard footsteps heading her way.

She searched quietly as she could for a weapon. She always carried her knife with her.

But when she went into her pocket to grab it, she didn't feel her knife at all.

Just that wooden attempt at a "boat" Max had crafted.

She went to put it back in her pocket when she saw it tumble to the forest floor.

Saw it land at her feet.

She heard the footsteps stop.

So close to her now.

So close they could literally be the other side of the tree.

Her heart beat so fast and heavy that her body actually shook.

Her mouth was totally dry.

She needed to get out of this.

She needed to time it right.

She needed to run.

She kept still. The longer she kept still, the longer she thought she might actually be alone. That there might be nobody here anymore. That they might've walked away, and she might've just missed hearing them.

Nothing but the breeze of the trees.

The cawing crows.

She went to shuffle to one side, look over her shoulder, and see if she was alone when she heard the footsteps again.

And she didn't even turn back this time.

She just ran.

She ran fast. Between the trees. Between trees that seemed to be getting narrower and narrower by the second.

She didn't want to look over her shoulder. She didn't want to see.

But at the same time, she felt like she was being hunted down.

Like she was being chased.

She looked over her shoulder.

For a second, she swore she saw someone.

A dark figure, closing in.

Fuck.

She didn't want to look anymore.

She didn't like weakness, and she didn't like standing up for herself, but she had no other option but to run right now.

She turned back around, and it all happened so fast.

The tree before her.

Not being able to stop herself.

Slamming right into it. Hard.

Falling to the ground.

She tasted blood.

Felt splitting pain right down her face. Her head banging. Her chest tight.

She lay there on the ground, head spinning, a tooth loose, and she knew she had no time to mope. No time to waste.

Because someone was chasing her.

She looked around.

Saw trees.

Saw a squirrel jumping from one branch to another.

But she didn't see anyone around.

She didn't see anyone chasing her.

Just that dead body, fresh in her mind.

She clenched her fists. Heart racing even harder if that were even possible.

Then she stood up.

She went to turn around when she felt something, suddenly.

A hand on her shoulder.

That's when she let out a cry.

# CHAPTER EIGHT

"Aoife. It's okay. It's me. It's okay."

Aoife heard Max's voice, and an immediate shot of calm fell over her. She felt the warmth of his hands against her arms, saw him looking into her eyes, and she felt her heart begin to slow immediately. She took deep breaths in. Deep breaths right into her belly. She was okay. Max was here. She wasn't alone.

"What's happened? Your face. You look like you've been punched."

Right on cue, fear engulfed Aoife. The person chasing her. The person in the woods. And the body, too. The dead body.

She looked over her shoulder.

Looked at the trees, shaking in the breeze.

Looked at the little floaters bobbing around her vision, which always appeared when she was stressed.

She looked around for a sign of life.

But as much as she looked... she couldn't see a trace of anyone.

"There... there was someone chasing me. And there's a body. A body in the woods. I... I found it. And then I saw someone near it, and—"

"Slow down, Aoife," Max said. His words immediately calming, reassuring. "Just... just slow down. Tell me everything. From the start."

Aoife looked over her shoulder again. "If we get the hell away from here fast, I might be more in the mood for talking."

Max nodded. They walked back through the woods, back towards the estate, Max by her side. She told him everything. About wandering out here. About seeing the movement. Then the footprints. She told him about the body lying naked, ties around the poor bloke's ankles and wrists. She told him about seeing the movement in the bushes, then turning around and running away.

And Max listened. He listened to every word. And his face didn't for one moment twitch.

"We should go find the body," Max said as they reached the solitude of the edge of the woods.

"What?"

"If there's a body out there, we can't just leave it out there. We need to go find it."

Aoife felt a tension deep in her gut. Her head throbbed, both with the hangover from earlier today and the stress of everything that'd happened since. "I don't... I don't want to go back in there."

"You don't have to. Just tell me where it is, and I'll see to it."

"There's someone out there, Max."

"And they chased you. Right."

She sensed some cynicism and scepticism to his voice. And she didn't like it. It rubbed her up the wrong way. Because it implied something she didn't want to hear.

"What are you trying to say by that?"

"I'm just saying..."

"Saying what?"

Max sighed. "You... you had a lot to drink earlier. And you've been here before."

"This isn't like before," Aoife said. "I know what happened. I know what I saw—"

"You tried to drink fucking bleach earlier," Max said. "So excuse me if I'm not exactly all aboard with you being completely with it right now."

She didn't just hear his words, she felt them. And they stung. Bad.

Because she knew what had happened. And she knew what she'd seen.

And sure, she knew there'd been times in the past where after drinking, she'd heard things. Seen things that weren't there.

But this wasn't like that.

This was different.

"How dare you," Aoife said.

Max shook his head, rolled his eyes. "Aoife, I'm just asking you to entertain the possibility that—"

"I know what the hell I saw," Aoife said. "I know what the hell happened to me. And just because you're suddenly singing Kumbaya around fireplaces because you've finally got over your dead wife and kid doesn't mean you get to lecture other people."

She regretted the words the second they left her mouth. She didn't mean them.

She was just lashing out. Because being doubted like this, being judged like this, it hurt her.

Especially by someone she cared about so dearly.

He looked at her with those wide eyes. Stared right at her. His lips twitched like there were things he wanted to say that he was holding back. Repressing.

And then he just shook his head.

"Make your own way back. Take Rex with you. I'll go search for the body."

He walked past her without saying another word to her.

And she wanted to tell him to stop.

She wanted to tell him not to go.

She wanted to say sorry.

But in the end, as he walked past her, she could only watch.

"Max," she said. "I didn't mean—"

"Go back," he said. Without turning around. "Just... just go back. I'll find the body. And I'll make sure there's nobody out here. And I'm sorry for doubting you."

He walked, then. And she wanted to apologise for snapping. For saying what she said about his family. She didn't mean it. She didn't mean to lash out in the ways she did.

But then he walked out of sight, into the trees, and it was just her and Rex. Alone.

She looked at where he'd disappeared to.

Then she looked down at Rex, who whined, and then back at the estate.

"Come on," she said. The allure of alcohol drawing her away. "Let's get you home."

She looked over her shoulder into the trees.

There was no sign of Max at all.

Overhead, the red glow of sunset dissipated, and darkness grew.

# CHAPTER NINE

He stood in the middle of the trees and stared off into the distance.

He saw the pair of them. The man. The woman. The dog, too.

And then, in the distance, he saw the estate.

The community.

Butterflies danced around his stomach. What he was doing was risky. But it was the right thing to do. The only thing to do.

A gamble that had to pay off.

And if it did... the reward would be so, so worthwhile.

He took a deep breath.

And he braced himself.

He felt nervous.

Terrified.

And he felt so, so guilty.

But he knew what he had to do.

He knew *exactly* what he needed to do.

He cleared his throat.

And then, he walked towards the estate.

# CHAPTER TEN

Max stepped into the trees, and right away, he felt like something was off.

He couldn't really put his finger on it. Sure, it was dark, but he didn't mind the dark. Didn't creep him out like it crept so many people out. If anything, it made him feel comfortable. Calm, somehow.

But right now, it felt creepy as shit.

The trees looked like they were figures, moving in his visual field, dancing around. Every single sound—a squirrel clambering up a tree, the wind blowing—made him flinch. The darkness had come fast, and it was getting faster. And as much as he wasn't exactly scared of the dark, he felt distinctly, deeply uncomfortable about it right now.

And it made him wonder if Aoife was right.

If he was wrong for doubting her all along.

He thought of Aoife, and he felt some bitterness inside. Because what she'd said to him about his family... it wasn't pleasant to hear that shit. He knew she was only lashing out. Punishing him. And he got it. He really did. She was suffering. She was struggling. She didn't mean the things she said.

And he guessed he was wrong to question her sanity. Like, in a way, he didn't regret it because she *did* have form, especially recently.

But he shouldn't have thrown that at her. Should at least investigate first.

Hell, he just felt bad. Because Aoife meant a shitload to him. More than he could put into words.

And more than he'd ever expressed.

He walked through the darkness, knife in hand, listening for any sound. He used to walk these woods a lot at night when he lived on Beacon Fell. Long walks, alone. Felt at peace, in a way. At one with the trees. With the animals. With nature.

Sounded like soppy, sentimental shit. But it really meant something to him. Nature got him through a lot of shit in the early days when he was out here. Feeling alone. Made him feel not so alone, actually.

Made him feel like Kathryn and David were right there with him, in some way.

But it didn't feel like that right now. Didn't feel at all like that.

It felt like a ghostly presence was lurking. Haunting him. Following him.

And as much as he wanted to turn around and head back to the estate, he knew equally that he needed to try and find the body. Try and find whoever had chased Aoife through these woods.

But she hadn't given him any locations. All he had to go on were her footprints.

And that's all it seemed to be. *Her* footprints.

Which made him wonder even more.

He walked along, followed the footprints. Swore he heard movement to his left. Thought he saw someone there, within the trees. He looked over his shoulder. He knew the estate was back there. And that voice in his head told him he should go back down there. That he should get someone out here to help. Or just wait til morning, til it was light. This whole thing was beginning to feel more and more reckless by the minute. More and more dangerous.

He wasn't sure he was going down the wisest road here.

He went to stop. To turn around. To head back to the estate. He had horrible visions of something happening to Aoife and Rex on the way back. To going back to the estate and finding that she hadn't returned.

He had to go back. Had to stop walking. Couldn't just leave them.

Especially not on the note they'd left each other on. He couldn't bear to think of that as the end.

He went to turn when he heard a shuffling right behind him.

He stopped. Looked around.

And he saw something.

Something that made the hairs on the back of his neck stand right on end.

There was something there. Something behind the trees.

Something moving.

Some*one*.

He was still for a few moments. Wasn't sure he wanted to walk towards that movement. Wanted to just watch it. To monitor it. To make sure they hadn't seen him.

He saw it.

The dark figure, shifting behind the trees.

For a moment, he swore he heard a whisper somewhere behind him.

And as much as he didn't like admitting it, Max felt fear.

He walked to the left. Slowly. Tried to be as silent as possible. Tried not to make a sound. Just had to get out of these woods, now. He could look for the body tomorrow. He could monitor the situation tomorrow when more people were here with him.

Right now, he got the distinct feeling that someone was in here with him. And that this wasn't safe at all.

He picked up the pace. Waded through the trees.

But the movement around him seemed to intensify.

The whispers around him sounded like they were getting louder.

He tried to tell himself to be rational. That he was just afraid. That chances were, there was nobody around. Nobody following him. Nobody chasing him. Nothing like that.

But for Aoife to say it too... and for him to feel this now. It couldn't be coincidence. There had to be something in it.

He moved further and further into the darkness when suddenly he bumped into something beneath him.

Almost lost his footing and fell to the ground.

When he saw what it was, his stomach dropped.

There was someone lying on the forest floor.

Clearly the body of a man.

Naked.

Ties around his wrists and ankles.

And a puddle of blood surrounding him.

Max looked down at the body, sickness creeping up. An ominous sense surrounding him.

Aoife was right.

She was totally fucking right.

They were in danger.

They were all in danger.

He went to turn around when he saw someone standing opposite, right behind him, appearing out of nowhere.

"Ssh," the man said.

And before Max could do anything, he felt a smack across his head, then darkness surrounded him.

# CHAPTER ELEVEN

Aoife saw the estate right up ahead, and she stopped in her tracks.

It was pitch black now. The clouds were thick overhead, suffocating any light from the moon and stars. Everywhere was just so quiet. No sounds other than the breeze against the trees behind. The estate looked so sleepy up ahead. No sounds at all from there, either. Not even any coughing, which was a rarity lately.

But it wasn't the estate Aoife had her focus on.

She turned around and looked back at the trees.

The mass where the forest started was totally black. She had no idea how long she'd been walking, but the journey took longer than usual after her fall down the slope. She just wanted to get back. She just wanted to go to sleep. Maybe have a drink before she went to sleep. Actually, what the hell was she on about, "maybe?" She was almost certainly going to need a drink. When was the last time she'd got to sleep without a drink?

And what was she going to do when the day came when drink finally ran out?

Fuck. She didn't want to think about that right now.

But there was no way she was sleeping tonight without some kind of help, especially with Max out there.

She looked back, Rex by her side. She knew Max was in there somewhere. And she was growing worried. Worried for his safety. Building in concern. Because he'd gone in there in search of the body. But Aoife knew there was someone else in there. Someone had chased her. Whether Max doubted and questioned her sanity or not, that's exactly how it went down.

Sure, she might've seen things in the past, but she wasn't insane. She knew exactly what she'd seen and what had happened.

And right now, she worried about Max.

About what might happen to him, alone in there.

He was tough. Strong. But so was she.

The man she'd found with the ties around his ankles and wrists looked strong, too.

And yet, something bad had happened to him. Something had got him into that state.

Someone had done that to him. Absolutely no doubt about it.

She clenched her fists. On the one hand, she wanted to go back to the estate. To drink, and to relax, and to sleep. Max told her to go back. She should honour his wishes. Respect them.

But on the other hand... the more time rolled on, the more she was starting to think that wasn't the right idea. Wasn't the right move at all.

She couldn't just leave him in there.

She had to go after him.

Whether she liked it or not, she felt something with Max. A connection to him. A bond to him.

And as painful as that was to face up to, as painful as that was to accept, she felt it. And she couldn't push it away. Couldn't resist it. Couldn't hide from it.

She looked down at Rex. Saw the way he was glancing up at the woods. He hadn't stopped looking back ever since they'd left Max's side. And she felt that, too. She wasn't going to be able to just turn away. Wasn't going to be able to just pretend everything was normal.

She couldn't leave him.

She had to go back into the woods.

She had to find him.

And she had to get him out of there.

Even though he'd chosen to go in there. Even though that was his call.

They were a duo. And she couldn't face losing him.

She held her breath, and she walked towards the trees.

The second she started walking, she noticed something.

There was someone standing there.

Someone right at the edge of the woods.

Wait, no. Not standing.

Rushing over towards her.

She stared up the hill. Whoever it was, it looked like they were limping. Stumbling in her direction. Hard to tell if it was a man or a woman. But they didn't look in a good way.

The way they were running, they looked like they were wounded.

Or scared.

She stood there. Heart racing. Watched the figure get closer. Her fists tensed. Her mouth went dry.

And the closer they got, the clearer it became that this was a man.

It was a man, and he looked like Max.

What had happened to him?

What had he seen?

The man stumbled and staggered closer, and then something else happened. Something unusual and uncharacteristic, if this was how it looked.

Rex began to growl.

Aoife looked at Rex.

Then up at the man.

And as he got closer, as his face became clearer, something else hit Aoife.

This wasn't Max.

It was a tall, slim man with floppy dark hair, a patchy beard, and pasty skin. He had really prominent brown eyes. He must've been in his thirties, but it was hard to tell.

He was covered in blood.

"Please," he said, shaking with fear. "Help... help me. Please."

He staggered a few more steps towards Aoife.

And then the light in his eyes went out, and he fell to the ground.

## CHAPTER TWELVE

"So what are we going to do about him?"

Aoife stood in the old library with a few of the locals—people who considered themselves "council members". She hadn't made the best efforts to bond with those who were here, but she knew them by name. The old bloke, Sam. Big bushy beard. Something of a voice of reason amongst the community. Older guy, many people saw him as the moral compass here.

Then there was Kathy. Self-appointed council leader and de-facto leader of the estate group. She'd lived here for years. Nice woman. Seemed friendly enough. Didn't have the baggage of being linked to James in that battle six months ago. Everyone seemed to respect her judgement, even if she could be a little cutting and to the point sometimes.

And at the back of the room, the man lay there.

He was on the floor, over by the old talking books section, which in a world without power, wasn't seeing as much attention as the rest of the library. Covered up. Sleeping. Or unconscious, rather. He was covered in crusted blood. He breathed heavily, struggling like he'd been beaten badly, and there was blood on his lungs or something. She wanted to wake him up. They all wanted to wake him up and figure out who he was. Where he'd come from. What secrets he was hiding.

And beyond that, Aoife wanted to know what had happened to Max—and if this man was anything to do with that.

"We have to wake him," Aoife said.

Sam shook his head. "The bloke looks like he's been to hell and back. Last thing we should do right now is disturb him."

"He might know something about Max," Aoife said. "And about the man I found in the woods."

"Aoife has a point," Kathy said, a little louder than Sam's careful whisper. "We have to know what kind of people we're bringing into our community. And besides. If Max really is in danger, then time is of the essence."

Aoife nodded, feeling somewhat vindicated. After all, they couldn't sit around wasting time. They had to get out of here. They had to go. Time was of the essence.

But at the same time... this man might know things they needed to know.

"Hey," Aoife said. Loud.

The man shuffled.

Sam frowned. "Aoife—"

"Hey!" she shouted. No time to waste. Walked right over to him. Shook him.

For a moment, Aoife wasn't sure the man was going to wake up. She thought he might be in a deep state of unconsciousness.

But then he gasped. Tried to swat Aoife away like he was amid a bad dream, and his nightmare had carried over into reality.

"They're coming," he gasped. "They come for everyone. For all of us. Not safe. Not—not safe!"

"Hey," Aoife said, holding his shoulders rather tightly. "You're okay. We've got you."

"I'm not okay. Nobody's okay."

"Stop speaking in riddles, okay?" Aoife said. "Who are you? Where'd you come from? And who were you running from?"

"Maybe go a bit easier," Sam muttered. "Don't bombard the man."

But the man looked around the candlelit library room with wide eyes. Looked from Aoife to Sam, to Kathy, then back round again. Rex sat in the far corner of the room, just watching over everything.

"Let's start with a name," Aoife said.

The man nodded. Took a few very audible deep breaths, breaths that smelled rather sour. "Vincent," he said.

"Vincent?"

"Vincent Cooper. Yourself?"

"My name doesn't really matter."

"She's called Aoife," Sam interrupted. "I'm Sam. And this here is Kathy. You're not our prisoner, as much as Aoife might be doing all she can to convince you otherwise. That's just... how she is with other people. Don't take it too personally."

Aoife tensed her jaw. Her head throbbed. Max was out there, and they didn't have time to waste. Especially when they didn't even know who the fuck this guy was.

"Vincent," Aoife said. "What happened to you? And give us the short version if you don't mind. Time's kind of of the essence here."

Vincent closed his eyes. Shook his head. It looked like he was revisiting a scene he didn't want to watch. Replaying something over in his head. "I... I was out there with my family. My brother, Wallace. His wife, Patty. And their children. Their... their two children."

"Cut to the chase," Aoife said. Fully realising she sounded unsympathetic, but also fully realising time was of the essence.

"Aoife," Sam said, tutting.

"We were travelling. Travelling through the woods. First, Patty went missing. Then the children. Then... then Wallace. And then it was just me. It was just me, until... until..."

"Until what?"

"They snook up on me," he said. "Captured me. Tortured me. Beat me. I don't know how long I was with them. But these people... they're savages. And they're close. So close."

Aoife felt a chill fall on the room. Felt a shiver creep down her spine amidst the silence.

"I managed to escape. But they're out there. They're—they're close. And they won't stop. They won't let me go. They—they won't ever let me go. They're in the woods, and they won't stop."

Aoife swallowed a lump in her throat. All she could think about was Max. He was out there, and he was in danger.

And if they didn't get out there fast, he might meet the same fate.

"What do these people want?"

Vincent looked up at her, right into her eyes, and she saw total fear. "I don't know. But they... Whatever they want, it isn't good. Not after what they did to my people. And what they'll—what they'll do to yours. Because they're watching you. I've seen them watching you. They've got guns and knives and—and they've got armies. Entire armies. And—and they're coming for you too. Soon. Very—very soon. They're—they're already coming."

Aoife looked around at Kathy. At Sam. Both of them looked paler than before as the light inside the library flickered away.

"But there's somewhere out there," Vincent said.

Aoife turned around. Frowned. "What?"

"The—the place we were heading to. Me and my family. Before... before they went missing. We were heading somewhere."

"Heading where?"

"It doesn't matter now. It's gone. All of it's gone."

"Vincent," Aoife said. "Where were you heading?"

He looked up into her eyes, and for a moment, the clarity returned.

"A safe place," he said.

Aoife frowned. "A safe place?"

"An—a safe zone. A place where there's army. A place where there's military. A place… a place where there's *power.*"

# CHAPTER THIRTEEN

Aoife stood at the door to the library, Sam and Kathy by her side, and she knew there was a very important discussion to be had about what they were going to do next.

It was dark. Pitch black. The thick of night now. She had no idea what time it was. No idea they'd been standing around debating what to do. No idea how long Max had been out there, either. Only he was in trouble. He was in danger. He would surely be back by now if he were okay.

She couldn't stop thinking about what Vincent said. About the group who captured his people. Him. Picked them off, one by one.

How they were out there. How they were close.

But also about this safe haven.

"What are we going to do?" Kathy asked.

Aoife looked around at her. She had a bad feeling about Kathy's approach. A bad feeling that her pragmatism—where she typically might actually agree with her—might put them at odds this time.

Because, like it or not, she had an attachment to Max. An attachment she didn't intend to betray.

"We have to go out there," Aoife said. "We have to go after Max. We have to find out where these people are Vincent's talking about, and we have to stop them. It's as simple as that."

She saw Kathy's face. The way she smiled at her like a disappointed teacher. Like there was still more to be said.

"But the place," Kathy said. "The safe haven he was heading towards."

"Are you really suggesting what I think you're suggesting?"

"People are tired, Aoife," Kathy snapped. "People are hungry. Resources are beyond thin. People are dying of sickness and starvation. We don't have much longer left. The people here need something. Anything."

"And Max is one of those people."

She opened her mouth as if to say something again. Then closed it. Sighed. "I know, Aoife. I understand. It's... it's not easy, letting people go."

"This isn't about what's easy or difficult. It's about what's right and wrong. And it's wrong to leave Max in the woods. Especially when these people are out there—"

"Then what would you have us do? Send our armies out there? Our unarmed armies? Starving, dehydrated armies? How many more would you see die just so you can save the only person you've bothered to care about?"

Aoife wanted to snap back at that. She wanted to put Kathy in her place.

She could see how Sam looked at her and Kathy. The way he lowered his head like he didn't want to chip in or suggest anything, because he feared he might upset the apple cart.

"That's... that's not what this is about."

"You've barely spoken a productive word in the six months you've been here," Kathy said. Clearly on one now. "And the only time you actually stand up and care about this place, it's because your one friend's gone missing. And now you're suggesting something reckless. Really reckless. I'm sorry about Max, Aoife. Really. I am. But... but I just don't see what good going to war will be. Sending people to their deaths. What use is that, really?"

Aoife lowered her head. She knew Kathy was right. That was the hardest thing. Logistically. Pragmatically. She was right.

They had to get out of this place. And if there was promise of some kind of safe haven on the horizon, then that's where they needed to go.

The survival of this very group depended on it.

She looked over at Sam. She wanted some kind of backup. Some kind of olive branch. Some sign that they weren't just going to throw in the towel. That they weren't just going to give up.

But Sam shrugged. "Maybe... maybe when we get to this place, if it's as good as Vincent says it is, they can help us. They can help us find Max again. But right now... I just don't see how we can."

Aoife felt a punch to the gut. Her last ally, and her only hope. The voice of reason of the group. And even he was going against her word.

"We go to this safe haven," Kathy said. "It's like Vincent said. It's not far away. And if we don't leave soon... we might be endangering everyone here. We wait til morning. And then we leave. That's how it has to be."

And Aoife wanted to argue. She wanted to contradict Kathy. To go against her orders.

But in the end, she could only look over at Rex and nod.

"It's the only thing we can do," she said. "For the community."

Kathy nodded. Put a hand on her arm. Lightly. Smiled.

"Come on," she said. "Get some rest. I doubt I'll be sleeping much. Doubt any of us will. But we're going to need to be at full strength tomorrow."

Aoife nodded. Thought of the allure of alcohol. How it might cure her problems and send her into unconsciousness.

She looked over at Vincent, who lay at the far side of the library.

Then she turned around and headed out into the darkness.

She knew what she had to do.

## CHAPTER FOURTEEN

Aoife stood at the gates of the estate in the dark of night. It was cold. A real chill in the air, even though it was summer. Up ahead, beyond the gates, she could see the dark outlines of the trees covering the hills. Just looking at them made her feel nervous. Sent a shiver right down her spine. She didn't want to go back out there. She didn't want to face what she'd faced the last time she was out there.

The body of the man.

And then the figure chasing her through the woods.

But on the other hand... a bitter taste filled her mouth. She felt guilty. Guilty for allowing Max to walk into those woods on his own. Guilty for the last words she said to him. The way she'd snapped at him.

She shook her head. She didn't want to think about what she'd said. She was guilty enough as it was.

She just knew there was only one way she could remedy things.

Only one thing she could do.

She looked down at Rex, panting by her side. She felt sorry for him, dragging him out there, into the woods, especially when something could happen out there. Something bad.

But then she guessed Rex wouldn't see it that way. He'd just see it as a nice walk. An adventure.

That's exactly how she had to frame it for him.

She looked back around, then. Back at the estate. At the terraced houses lining the streets. At the old shops that had been boarded up for months. At the library, where Vincent was. She looked over there, and she thought of the fear in his voice. The way he'd looked at her, looked at them all, terrified, covered in blood.

Whoever he'd managed to escape, they weren't good news.

And from everything he'd said, they were exactly the same people who had left the man in the woods.

Exactly the same people who Max would be in danger from right now.

She tightened her fists. She had a blade in her pocket. It wasn't much, but it was something.

But looking back at the estate, she expected to feel sadness about what she was going to do. Some kind of trepidation about leaving this place. Because it was her home. And it had been her home for six months now.

But looking back at these streets, she realised just how alien they felt. How abnormal they felt. And she realised she had never felt at home on these streets. Not really.

Her home was in those woods.

Her home was Max now.

She turned around, ruffling Rex's fur, and she took a long breath.

"Come on, Rex," she said. "Let's get ourselves out of here. Let's go find your dad."

She braced herself.

Then, she took a step out of the confines of the estate.

Into the unknown.

## CHAPTER FIFTEEN

Max opened his eyes, and he knew right away he was in deep shit.

It was dark. Or was he blindfolded? He didn't know. Couldn't tell. He felt cold. Shivery all over. For a moment, he thought it might be bloody winter. But then he remembered the suffocating warmth of summer they'd all been living through at the estate and came right back to reality.

He tried to look around, tried to squint into the darkness, but it was impossible to see a thing. He could hear things. Muffled sounds. Like voices. Like people were trying to speak to him, but he couldn't hear them, couldn't make out their words. The whole room, or wherever he was, smelled bad. Really bad. Like piss and shit and a whole host of awful things all mixed together and turned up a notch. His mouth was dry and tasted of blood. His wrists and ankles were sore. Really sore. Binds tied right around them, really tight.

He tried to squint again, tried to see through that surrounding darkness. But he realised there must be something over his face. Covering his stinging eyes. Where was he? What was this?

He tried to think back. To remember exactly what had

happened to put him here. He'd gone after Aoife to try and find her. Found her in the woods, running from something. They'd had a pretty heated standoff, and then he'd gone off into the woods to try and find this body she was talking about.

After some scepticism, he'd found it.

And then someone had approached him and...

A thump against Max's head, the last thing he remembered.

Although... there were other things, too. Vague memories. Memories of being carried somewhere. Of people holding him, their hands tight around him. Someone telling someone else to be careful.

*"Don't hurt him. That's the last thing we want to do..."*

He remembered hearing that caution, that care, in the voices of those carrying him away, and it sent a shiver up his spine. Gave him the creeps.

There was something off about the people who'd captured him. Something different about them. He just couldn't put his finger on what it was.

He tried to edge forward. His wrists and ankles were tied, but his body wasn't pinned back to anything. He was able to shuffle around whatever space he was in. It felt open. Cold. Some kind of warehouse?

Fuck it. Didn't matter. Not really.

He just had to get the hell out of here—and fast.

He went to shuffle forward. To edge forward. To get the hell away from wherever the hell he was.

His head banged against something solid and sharp. Metal, from the sounds of things. He stumbled. Tried to keep his footing, then tripped back, hit the ground.

As he hit the ground and lay there, heart racing, he realised he'd landed on something somewhat soft. Like some kind of bedding. And again, it made him feel weird. Made him feel uneasy. It's like whoever had put him in here was trying to stop him hurting himself. Trying to cushion his fall.

And again, that just made him feel like something was *off*.

He lay there a few seconds. Heart racing. He needed to be calm. Needed to take things easy.

He needed a plan.

He didn't want to go acting rash. He knew damn well acting rash never got anyone anywhere. He was all about pragmatism and always had been.

"Come on," he muttered to himself. "You can get yourself out of this. You can..."

He realised something, then.

The ties around his wrists.

They were where he needed to start.

If he could get back to that sharp metal edge he'd walked into, then he could try to break through the ties around his wrists.

If he could break free of those, he could get his blindfold off.

He could get his ankle ties away.

He stood up. Slowly. A little wobbly on his feet. Walked over towards the metal he'd banged into. Trying to find his footing. Not even sure whether he was heading in the right direction, but hopeful.

And a weird sense that time was of the essence.

That he needed to hurry.

Because he wasn't alone.

He crept further and further towards the metal gate when he bumped against it.

His heart raced. This was the one. This was the one he'd walked into before. It had to be.

He searched it slowly. With cold, frozen fingers. Those muffled noises, like voices, still noisy in the background.

He kept on searching it, heart racing, feeling like time was running out.

And then he felt it.

The sharp edge on the gate, sticking right out.

Elation filled his body. Relief and adrenaline surged through. He was getting out of this. He was getting the hell out of this.

He pushed his wrist ties against it. Moved them up and down, scraping them against the sharp metal. Trying to break through the ties.

"Come on," he muttered. "You're almost there. Come on."

He felt the sharp metal scratching against his wrist. Swore he felt blood trickling down his arm.

But he didn't care.

Just had to keep on trying.

Just had to keep going.

Just had to—

It all happened so quickly.

His wrists felt free.

He opened them up.

The ties dropped away.

He stood there for a few seconds, shaking, frozen. Still in disbelief that he'd actually got free of them.

And then he knew there was no more time to waste.

He dragged off his blindfold.

When the vision poured in, it took him a few seconds to really clock where he was. To really process the scene around him.

But when he looked around closely, it hit him.

He was in some kind of dirty, dark room. There was filthy stained bedding on the solid grey floors. The walls were covered in cracked tiles, which were once white but now had a clear brownish hue.

And all around him, he saw something that sent shivers up his spine.

There were people.

People with blindfolds over their eyes or coverings over their heads. Naked but for their underwear. Wrists and ankles tied, just like him.

Some of them shaking.

Some of them mumbling.

Some of them just lying there like they'd accepted their fate.

He crouched down. Heart racing. He pulled at the ties around his ankles. Stretched at them with all his strength. Tried to snap them, tried to break free of them.

"Come on," he said. "Come on..."

And then he heard something.

Footsteps.

Footsteps echoing towards him.

He pulled even harder at the ties.

Pulled as hard as he could.

But he was shaking too hard.

*Fuck. Pull yourself together. Come on.*

He pulled harder at them.

Heard footsteps getting closer.

The smells of this place growing more and more pungent.

The sounds of the muffled cries getting louder.

And the images of those people lying there, like they'd given up, haunting him.

He kept on pulling at the ties when finally, they split free.

Relief. Elation.

And adrenaline.

Because he knew what he needed to do now.

He knew where he needed to go.

He went to clamber his way out of this room he was in when right on cue, someone walked up to the metal gate before him.

Stood there.

Stared at him.

Cattle prod in hand.

He didn't have time to hesitate right now.

He threw himself towards the exit, right by the side of this man, the narrow gap beside him.

He landed face first just outside his prison.

He clambered to his feet. Just had to get away. Just had to run. Just had to—

A bolt of electricity surged down his spine, freezing him in his tracks.

Burning right through every inch of his body.

He tumbled to the floor, face first. Smacked his skull and tasted blood in an instant.

As he lay there, the electricity running through his body, burning him hotter and hotter, all he could see were more little pens like the one he'd been trapped in.

More of them, with more people inside.

As he looked around, totally paralysed, Max realised exactly what this place was.

How fucking desperately he needed to get out of here.

And how much Aoife and the rest of the community needed to stay away from here.

Far, far away from here.

# CHAPTER SIXTEEN

Aoife stepped into the woods and regretted coming back here right away.

It was dark. Even darker than she thought was possible. She had no idea what time it was anymore, only that it had to be the early hours, getting towards morning. Everything was so quiet. Everything felt so intimidating.

And it felt like someone was in here with her. Watching.

She looked around at the trees through the gaps. She kept on seeing movement, but it was mostly just the floaters in her eyes. Her mind playing tricks.

At least that's what she told herself to feel better, anyway.

Shit. She wished she'd had a drink before she came out here. Might've made this whole process a bit easier for her. Definitely would've given her a little Dutch courage. Something that had carried her through a lot of shit these last few months.

But she was here now, so there was no point complaining.

She just had to find a trace of Max.

Find *any* trace of Max.

It was the only thing she could do.

She heard panting, the only sound amidst the silence. Looked down, saw Rex there beside her. She'd brought him along for two reasons. Kind of torn initially. Didn't want to put him in any danger. She loved the damned dog, after all.

But she'd brought him along for company and also because if there was a trace of anyone—or if there was a trace of *Max* anywhere—he'd get a scent of him before she did.

"You okay, lad?"

He didn't look at her. Just sniffed the air. Wagged his tail a bit. Felt like he was on the scent of something. Felt like he knew something was close.

Or some*one*.

She walked further into the woods. The deeper she got, the darker it grew. She wasn't sure exactly where she'd found the body. She hadn't really had any direction in mind when she'd stumbled upon it. Wandering aimlessly, really. And that was making things difficult. Finding it again, rediscovering it.

But she figured if this group Vincent told her about was as active in these woods as he'd made out—if they really were the looming threat he said they were—she'd come across a trace of them eventually.

She'd find them.

And then she could follow them to Max.

She walked further and further through the woods until eventually, she noticed something.

A patch in the ground.

Sort of an indentation. Like someone or something had been here not long ago.

She stared at it, the hoot of an owl cutting through the silence, and she realised something.

This was where she'd fallen.

Where she'd tumbled down the slope trying to get away.

Her heart rate picked up a bit. She looked ahead, saw the prints where she'd fled. She'd made it. Found it. She was on the right track.

She had to follow those prints.

And then she'd reach the body.

And after that...

Who knows what she'd find?

She clambered up the slope. Slipped a few times. Took her a while to get to the top.

But when she got there, she saw the bush before her, and it all came flooding back.

The bush that she'd found the body behind.

This was it. It might be pitch black now, but without a shadow of a doubt, this was it.

She walked over towards it. Not sure what she was going to find when she got there.

She held her breath.

Stepped around the bush.

And she froze.

There was a patch on the ground. Hard to make out in the darkness of night, but quite clearly a patch of something reflecting the moonlight back.

Blood.

But there was no body.

She gulped. Her mouth was dry, totally dry. She felt the nerves kick in. Felt her head throbbing.

And for a moment, she wondered if she *had* imagined her discovery.

She wondered if Max's scepticism wasn't unfounded after all.

But then there was Vincent.

There was Vincent and the chase and what he'd said and—

Movement.

Shuffling, right behind her.

She spun around.

Looked into the darkness.

Nothing.

No movement.

No sounds.

Nothing.

But that unwavering sense that someone was here.

Someone was close.

Someone was watching.

She gritted her teeth. Realised her fingernails were buried deep into her palms.

By her side, Rex just stared. Didn't growl, just stared.

"Come on," she said, knowing she had to keep moving. "Let's keep going. No point staying here. We'd better..."

Then she heard it again.

And this time, she swore she saw it.

Movement.

Movement rushing across in front of her.

She looked into the darkness of the woods.

Her stomach turned.

And she was certain now.

She was certain that she wasn't alone.

That there was someone out here.

She wanted to go back. Wanted to get back to the estate. Didn't want to be out here, not anymore.

But then she thought of Max. How she couldn't leave him in here. Couldn't leave him behind.

She went to turn around and walk further.

She walked. And the more she walked, the more in uncharted territory she felt. The more intimidated she felt. She didn't even know if she was heading in the right direction. Didn't even know if Max was here at all.

Only that she had to keep on searching. She couldn't just give up.

She looked up at the sky. Slightly lighter. A dark blue, but better than the pitch black of before.

She looked back down and stopped.

Somebody was standing right there.

Right in front of her.
A dark figure.
And then, in her periphery, she saw more movement.
More figures in the dark.
She wasn't alone.

# CHAPTER SEVENTEEN

Aoife saw the figures surrounding her, and she knew she was in deep shit.

The night felt especially dark. Intense. Suffocating. Rex stood by her side, growling. But his ears were down. And he looked like he was shaking. Like even he was intimidated and afraid about this whole situation.

She could see the figures all around her. And it was pretty obvious they weren't visions or hallucinations. She could see them quite clearly.

And it seemed like they were everywhere she looked.

She turned around on the spot. She couldn't tell whether they were men or women. She couldn't tell whether they were armed or not. She couldn't tell a thing.

Just that she had to get the fuck away from them.

She had to get away.

Fast.

She turned around to run when she saw one of them standing right in front of her.

It was a woman. Long, ginger hair, illuminating slightly in the moonlight. She looked at Aoife with these sad eyes. And that's what stuck with Aoife more than anything else. The sad expression on her face. Not intimidating. Not menacing. Just... sad.

She was holding something.

Not a knife or a blade. Some kind of long prod.

"Don't make it hard for yourself, hun," she said. "There's no reason for this to be painful at all. I'm sorry you've run into us like this. Really, it's just bad luck. But you could really make the whole thing a lot easier on yourself if you just don't resist. Please."

She listened to these words, and again, it would make sense in her mind if they were coming from someone who sounded menacing. Who sounded... well, evil.

But she didn't. She sounded calm. Cool. Collected.

And genuinely apologetic.

The figures closed in. Rex barked, kicking back his paws. She could see three of them in front of her, stopping her from progressing. A couple by her side.

She looked over her shoulder, back towards the woods. Just one of them there.

Then back at the woman again.

"My friend," Aoife said, clenching onto the knife in her shaking hand. "Max. What the hell have you done with him?"

The woman sighed. Looked right down at the ground. "Let go, hun. Just let go. There's no point fighting. Not anymore."

It all happened so quickly.

Two of the figures lunged towards Aoife.

A spark of electricity flickered at the top of the pole the ginger woman was holding.

And she knew she had no other choice.

She swung around.

Ran.

Ran back towards the trees.

Heard them chasing her, close behind.

Heard Rex barking, running alongside her.

The figure—a man—blocking her way into the woods stood there.

Baseball bat in hand.

"Stop," he said. Again, assertively, not menacingly. "You're not making this easy on yourself."

But Aoife wasn't for talking.

She wasn't for sticking the fuck around here.

She lunged around the side of the man.

Towards the trees.

If she could just get there, get back into cover, she could hide. She could lay low. She could use the darkness as cover.

She just had to get there.

She just had to—

A hand against her shoulder.

Dragging her back to the ground.

She tumbled back. Slammed against the ground, right onto her back.

Rex barking at the man standing over her.

Baseball bat in his hand.

Behind, the oncoming people pursuing her closing in.

"Don't fight," the man said. "You're doing yourself a favour if you just don't—agh!"

He didn't see it. And Aoife barely even registered it herself. It was pure instinctive reaction.

Slamming the knife into his foot.

Burying it right through its centre.

Feeling the hot blood spurting out, right over her hand.

She tried to pull it back out as he stood there, screaming out.

But it was stuck. Completely stuck.

She let go.

"Come on, Rex. Come on!"

And then she ran.

She ran, Rex by her side.

Ran, the pursuing group right on her tail.

Ran until she reached the trees.

Until the darkness covered her again.

She didn't look back. Didn't stop for anything. Just kept going. Just kept running. There wasn't a thing else she could do. Even though it wasn't going to get her any closer to Max.

There was no getting to Max right now.

There was no hope on that front.

She ran and ran until she suddenly saw someone standing in front of her, just up ahead.

She stopped. Slowed right down. Right behind, she could hear feet pelting against the ground. Chasing her. Closing in.

She held her breath. Crept off, over to the thick bushy area. She crouched down there, with Rex by her side. She held him. Stroked his head. Kept on holding her breath. Not sure how long she could hold it. Just that she needed to stay here. Needed to stay quiet. Couldn't let them see her.

She saw the figure moving through the darkness, right towards where she'd come. And then she saw the rest of the group appear. Four of them, by the looks of things. Seemed like more of them back up there, but it was hard to tell. She could still hear shouting at the top of the hill. Shouting from the guy she'd stabbed. Cutting through the night.

She lay there on the ground. Heart beating so fast she felt like she was shaking the earth.

Watched as those figures got closer.

And closer.

Held on to Rex.

Waited for them to reach her.

Waited for the end...

"Hey, Dean?" a bloke shouted. "Stay away from those trees. You know the boss keeps his traps near places like that."

The man stopped. She could see him looking so close to her.

Then he sighed and walked away.

Aoife stayed there, lying on the ground. She stayed there,

totally still. Shaking. Right beside her, she saw the leg-hold trap. So close.

She wasn't sure how long she lay there, but it must have been a while because the sky started to lighten, and the orange glow of the sun began to rise.

And as Aoife lay there, staring into the woods, she knew there was only one thing she could do.

She had to get up.

She had to go back home.

Because this was beyond Max.

This was way, way beyond just Max now.

# CHAPTER EIGHTEEN

"Are you sure this can't have waited til morning, Aoife?"

Aoife sat in Kathy's living room, holding on to a glass of water that she had no intentions of drinking whatsoever. She was shaking. Felt freezing cold like she had the worst hangover in the world. She hadn't slept a wink, but she wasn't exhausted—she was wired.

And as she sat in Kathy's living room, all she could think about was that group in the woods.

The sense of dread she had about Max and what had happened to him.

And also the sense that they needed to be careful here. Because something didn't feel right. Something just didn't feel right at all.

"It can't," Aoife said. Kathy's living room looked like a real pre-EMP living room in all truth. Flowers on the windowsill, sickly sweet to smell. A television in the corner of the room, surprisingly dust-free considering it was a useless item in a post-power world. And loads of frames on the walls with cheery, motivational quotes staring down at her. The kind that always made Aoife's stomach turn a little.

*Live. Laugh. Love.*

*You Are Living Your Story.*

Fucking vom.

Kathy sighed. She looked exhausted. Big bags under her eyes. "Tell me again exactly what happened."

Aoife went through it all again. Going out into the woods to search for Max. The sudden appearance of the figures. The way they'd surrounded her.

And how calmly that woman spoke to her.

How cool and detached she'd sounded.

"Something just feels... off," Aoife said.

Kathy sipped her brew. "The way I see it, it's further proof we need to leave here as soon as possible."

"But..."

"Are you suddenly objecting to leaving this place? You've changed your tune."

"I just... This group. There were plenty of them. But they didn't seem well-armed. And they didn't seem as Vincent described them."

"Do you doubt Vincent?"

Aoife opened her mouth. Did she doubt Vincent? "Well, we don't know a lot about him. Where he came from. What his agenda is. Just that he shows up out of nowhere talking about some mysterious safe place. Right when we're at our weakest. Trying to lure us out of this place, into the open. I don't know. Don't you think we should just be careful before we go jumping into anything?"

Kathy shook her head. "I understand. Really, I do. But we're not exactly well equipped here, Aoife. And we can't exactly be taking any chances right now."

"But this is taking a chance," Aoife said. "I've... I've seen what these people are like. They're more like... like less well-armed than an army. And I just don't know. Something isn't right. There's lots of them, but they're not what I expected. Something's off. Really off. And I don't know what it is."

"You've picked a funny time to start caring," Kathy said.

Aoife frowned. "What?"

"Don't take this the wrong way. But you haven't exactly been the most... sensitive member of this community for the last six months."

"I—"

"And while I appreciate the sudden concern, I can't help wondering if it's related to the only person around here you seem to genuinely care about, somehow."

Aoife lowered her head. Max. She'd gone out there to try and find him, and she'd failed to even find a trace of him. She'd ended up back here, tail between her legs, and left with more questions than answers.

But Kathy was wrong about something.

"I... I do care," Aoife said. "I just... It's hard. Making connections. When you just lose them anyway in this world."

Kathy stood up. "Aoife, sweet. That's the way the world's always been. It's not new to this world."

Aoife looked up at Kathy. Deep down, she knew she was right. "I'm just worried about what might happen if we leave this place. And also worried—"

"What might happen if we *don't* leave this place. I get it. I know. But the way I see it, we've only got one choice. This place... it's already gone. The people out there, the group, they've only accelerated a decision we were already going to have to make. There isn't anything here for us. There's no resources. There's nothing close by enough to sustain us. It's time we moved on. And with the talk of the safe haven... it's the only thing we can do."

"And you believe in that place?" Aoife asked.

"What?"

"The safe haven Vincent speaks of. You really believe in it?"

Kathy opened her mouth. Then she closed it again. "I have to.

We all have to. Because if we don't... what else is there for any of us?"

She walked past Aoife. Over to the curtains of her front room. Stood by the window, looked outside as the sun continued to rise. As the orange glow filled the estate's streets.

"I want to stay here," Kathy said. "It's a beautiful thing we've built, and I don't want to lose that. But at the same time... we need to evolve. We need to adapt. Or we won't survive. We won't stand a chance. We're already at our absolute limit as it is. Don't you see that?"

Aoife knew Kathy was right, deep down. But she just had a bad feeling about the whole thing.

And there was something else, too.

The thought of reaching this place.

The thought of settling into somewhere new, with new people.

People she was going to get close to.

People she would inevitably lose.

The thought of it made her feel physically sick.

"I'm sorry about Max," Kathy said. "Wherever he is... I truly believe we'll see him again. And I truly believe he'd be fully on board with what we are doing, too. And it *is* what we are doing."

Aoife wanted to argue. To protest.

But then Kathy spoke before she could.

"We are leaving this place. Before the outsiders attack. And we are leaving this morning, first thing. It's time, Aoife. Time for a new beginning. And nothing is stopping that."

## CHAPTER NINETEEN

Aoife looked out at the woods in the distance and felt all the hairs on the back of her neck stand right on end.

It was morning. She hadn't slept a wink. She felt rough as hell, even rougher than if she'd spent the entire previous night drinking. A sure-fire advert for drinking, that was for sure.

She'd sat on her sofa, Rex at her feet, and thought about Max constantly. Thought about going out there again. Trying to find him.

But knowing that wasn't an option.

This place was in danger.

An imminent threat was heading their way. She'd seen it. First-hand.

They had to get to the safe haven Vincent spoke about, whether Aoife liked it or not.

She felt a warm summer breeze brush against her skin. Her hair shuffled in the wind. She looked around and saw the residents of the community all standing around. All forty or so of them. All here, all outside the gates. An unprecedented gathering.

She saw faces she recognised. And faces that were barely familiar. And it struck her that really, these people were all strangers to her, but that's because she'd never really made any attempts to connect with them. To bond with them.

For good reason. Didn't need any more friends. Didn't need any more connections. She'd had all the connections she needed already. That chapter in her life was well and truly over.

She looked over to the left, over to the grassy area beyond the gates. The graveyard, where she could just about see the wooden crosses peeking over. She thought of Nathan lying there. Of Moira lying there. The reminder of that day. Of everything that had happened. And how much everything had changed—her entire life had changed.

She swallowed a lump in her throat and turned back around.

Up top, she could see Kathy. By her side, Vincent. He was talking to her, pointing into the distance. He looked more confident now. Taller than she expected, now she was finally seeing him on his feet. Calmer, too. But with an air of excitement—an air of excitement about this safe place he was leading them towards.

Every now and then, he looked over at Aoife. She didn't keep eye contact with him, though. Didn't want to risk connecting with someone else.

Just get the hell to somewhere safer and then get finding Max. That's all she cared about. Wasn't here to make friends.

She heard footsteps behind her, then someone clearing their throat.

"You okay?"

She looked around. Not expecting someone to be speaking to her. After all, why would anyone speak to her?

When she turned, she saw a bloke called Amir standing there. He was a pretty good-looking guy in all truth. Long, curly dark hair. Really nice brown eyes and a gorgeous smile.

She looked over her shoulder to check he wasn't speaking to someone else, which somehow seemed more likely. When she looked back, she realised he was definitely speaking to her.

"Yeah, you. Aoife, right?"

Aoife felt herself blushing a bit. Which embarrassed her even more and made her frigging blush even more. She wasn't used to getting embarrassed, especially around blokes.

But she'd changed a lot this last six months. Her confidence wasn't exactly sky-high. A loner who drank herself to sleep every night. She wasn't exactly a catch, was she?

"Yeah," she said. "That's me."

"Sorry to hear about Max," Amir said. "That must be really rough to take."

She looked up at him. A bolt of anger shot through her. "He's —he's not dead. He's still out there. I'm not giving up on him."

Amir held his hands up. "Hey. I'm sorry. I didn't mean anything by it. I just mean... Look. This is a lot for all of us today, right? The stuff about the group out there. And this safe haven. It's a lot to digest. I'm just saying... I'm sorry. I don't know what I'm trying to get at, really. Sorry."

He walked past her, head lowered, shoulders slumped. And she felt bad. Bad for firing him off. After all, what were people supposed to think? That Max had gone on a nice country walk, and he was going to rock up absolutely fine?

She knew it was mad to even assume that.

And that's why this whole leaving process was even harder on Aoife.

Because as much as she wanted to believe Max was still out there... she had to look at the evidence before her—evidence she'd seen quite clearly herself—and recognise that was unlikely.

"I'm sorry," she said.

Amir stopped. Turned around. "Did someone say something?"

"Don't be a dick about it," Aoife said. "I... I'm sorry, okay? It's just... Well. It's like you said. This is... this is a lot. For all of us."

She didn't look Amir in the eye when she spoke. But when she finally did glance up, she saw he was standing there, a smile on his face.

"We've never properly spoken before," he said.

"There's not a lot to say."

"Somehow I doubt that."

She saw the way he looked at her, a little longer than was appropriate.

And a part of her wanted to ask him to walk with her. To keep her company on their journey.

A part of her desperately wanted that company.

But then Kathy started speaking, and he turned around, and everyone turned around to stare at her, to listen.

She stood there. Right at the front of the group. Vincent by her side, looking sheepish as ever. A pale, gaunt expression across her face.

"Today isn't going to be easy," Kathy said. "It could well be dangerous. But we stick together, and we make it. We don't know what we might find out there. But we can only know for definite that it has to be better than the place we've called home. Home served a purpose. The estate here and the community we've built... it's a beautiful thing. But resources are waning. Our rations are running thin. Sickness is ravaging us. And we should have no shame in admitting we've reached the limits of our own potential. It's time for us to move forward. All of us. It's time for us to move on. To seek help."

She looked around. Her cheeks flushed a bit like she was uncomfortable with all the attention.

She cleared her throat again. "Home..." she said. Tensing a fist and pressing it to her chest. "Home is... home is right here. Not there. But right here. And it's in all of us."

She blushed even more at that. And Aoife felt herself blushing for her, too, even though plenty of people were clapping.

"Damn."

A voice. Right by Aoife's side.

She looked around. Saw Amir.

"That line about home being right here," he said. "Did she

really have to do that to us? Did she really have the bring the cringe? Really?"

And as much as Aoife didn't want to mock Kathy, as much as she didn't want to feel anything but remorse for Max, anything but fear... she couldn't help laughing.

"Now come on," Kathy said, looking at Vincent, then at the rest of the group. "Let's say our goodbyes. Let's leave this place. And let's go find our new home."

# CHAPTER TWENTY

Aoife walked into the outskirts of the woods with the rest of her group and couldn't shake the sense that something was going to go horribly wrong.

It'd turned out a stuffy, muggy morning. Cloudy and sweaty. What she'd give for a proper shower. Or a relaxing bath. The luxury of lavender bubbles soaking her tired limbs. That soothing floral scent in the air. That gentle sound of the bubbles individually popping.

And then the feeling of a blister bursting on her foot, making her stumble, sending her crashing back down to earth.

They were right on the outskirts of the woods. Thick green trees peered down at them. Aoife kept on looking up there, into the darkness beyond. She kept on thinking back to the early hours, just a matter of hours ago really. To going back in there in search of Max. To running into that group. How ominous it all felt. How *off* it all felt.

It was so quiet in there. And yet, at the same time, the silence was deafening, cliche as it may sound. Birdsong. Wind. The branches and the leaves dancing against one another like the woods itself was alive.

And that constant feeling that she was being watched.

That they were all being watched.

But hey. Safety in numbers, right? That's what she had to keep on telling herself. That's what she had to believe.

She took in deep breaths of that warm, clammy air. The smell of summer. The reminder of the walks she used to go on with Jason, goddamn him. They'd go up to the Lakes and disappear off the trail. End up in all kinds of untouched, relatively undiscovered locations. Once, they'd come across a whole family of deer, going about their business. One of the most beautiful scenes Aoife had ever witnessed.

And yet the saddest thing about it?

The thought that if they came across a gorgeous family of deer now, her first instinctive thought—everyone's first instinctive thought—would be what a great capture it would be. What a great source of food it would be.

She kept her focus ahead. Walked alone, only Rex for company. She was happy that way. She just wanted to get to this safe haven. The sooner they got there, the sooner she could inform whoever ran the place—military, Vincent suggested—about Max.

Because as much as logic told her there was no finding him... she couldn't just roll over and accept that. She couldn't just admit defeat like that.

She had to believe there was still a chance.

She had to believe there was still hope.

"Never liked these woods."

Aoife jumped. Looked around. Saw Amir appearing beside her out of nowhere. "You've got to stop sneaking up on me like that."

Amir smirked. "Sneaking up on you? We're in a group of forty. It's not like you're on a lone trek through the wilderness here."

Aoife sighed, looked away. He was starting to irritate her, but in a way she couldn't explain. She *wanted* to walk with him. She wanted to *talk* with him.

But at the same time, there was this huge mental hurdle stopping her from doing that.

Like something was standing in her way. In the way of attachment. In the way of connecting with other people.

Fear.

"I'd rather just walk alone," Aoife said.

Amir frowned. "Oh."

"Sorry. I don't mean to be rude. I'm just—"

"No, it's fine. Whatever. I mean, yeah. Bit rude. But it doesn't matter."

"I didn't ask to speak to you. Just respect it and walk on."

Amir frowned. Looked slightly pissed off now. "What happened to you to make you like this?"

Aoife felt a surge of rage run through her. She wanted to explode. He had no idea what'd happened to her. The loss she'd felt. The things she'd been through. He had no idea at all.

"I'm sorry about your friend," he said. "I liked Max. He was... he's a good guy. I hope he shows up. But whatever. You don't want to talk."

He walked on. And Aoife still hadn't quite cooled down when she felt another presence beside her.

"You should go a bit easier on him."

She turned, ready to lambast someone else—anyone else who got in her way today—when she saw Sam standing there.

Sam was the elder of the group if such a term was appropriate. The bloke who was there with Kathy and her the night she'd taken Vincent back. He was always kind. Didn't poke his nose into too much. And Aoife respected him for keeping his distance.

"Maybe he should go a bit easier on me," Aoife said.

Sam shrugged. "I'm just saying. I'm not negating what you've been through. Not belittling you in any way. But... well. Do you even know Amir's story?"

Aoife opened her mouth, and she realised in an instant just

how terrible she felt for almost uttering the words "I don't care." Was that what she'd turned into? What she'd become?

"I'm not asking you to be friends with anyone," Sam said. "I'm just asking you to be a little more conscious and a little more aware that... respectfully, you aren't the only one who is dealing with things. You aren't the only one who has suffered loss. Great, great loss."

He didn't say anything else. Just drifted over to another small group. And suddenly, walking alongside Rex, Aoife felt alone. Very alone.

And she felt guilty, too.

Guilty and ashamed about how she'd spoken to Amir. Because Sam was right. She had no idea what anyone else had been through because she hadn't *wanted* to know what anyone else had been through.

She hadn't wanted to care.

Because caring just opened herself up to being hurt.

She looked ahead. Saw Amir walking up ahead. And as much as she felt resistance inside, she walked a little quicker towards him.

That's when she heard it.

Right at the front of the group.

A scream.

# CHAPTER TWENTY-ONE

Aoife heard the scream, and immediately, every hair on her body stood on end.

It came from the front of the group somewhere. Hard to make out where exactly because of the trees, and the people ahead of her, distorting just how far ahead everything was.

She wanted to go up there. Wanted to see what the fuck was going on. Because the screaming was getting louder. It sounded like someone was in pain. In serious pain.

And all she could think about were the people in the woods.

The way they'd chased her.

And how wrong all of this felt.

She felt torn. Torn between wanting to hold her ground and between investigating. Checking what was going on up there. As much as she didn't want to face it. As much as she wanted to run far from it.

But in the end, instinct reigned supreme.

"Fuck it," she said.

She ran. Ran towards the front of the group. Ran past the mass of confused and terrified people. Some of them running along with her. Others stepping back. All of them dissipating in different directions. The group fragmenting. Splitting up.

She reached the front of the group, and she heard the scream again.

But she couldn't figure out where it was coming from.

She couldn't see anyone suffering.

Anyone in pain.

She looked at Kathy, who stood there, staring ahead.

Then at Vincent, who was muttering things under his breath.

"It's them," he muttered. "It's—it's them."

Aoife looked ahead and saw the source of the scream.

It came from the woods, right up ahead. A thickened area of woodland. And that scream. It was so loud. She couldn't see who it was coming from, but she could hear the pain. She could hear the distress.

Vincent panted. Sweating like mad. Staring into space. "It's—it's them. This is how they operate. We need to go. We need to get away. We need to get away!"

Aoife looked at Kathy, who looked back at her, clearly at a loss about what to do.

And then she looked around at the woods.

The hair on the back of her neck stood on end. Because it felt like there were eyes on her. Like there were people here.

Watching.

She heard that scream again and looked ahead.

"What do we do?" Kathy asked. Behind, Aoife could hear commotion building up. People were moving in both directions. The group were being split up.

Aoife looked at the source of the scream.

Readied herself.

Then she stepped forward.

"Be careful," Kathy said. "Be..."

Aoife didn't hear anything else.

She stepped beyond the bush.

Into the darkened area of woods.

It didn't take long at all for her to find the source of the scream.

She saw someone right away.

There was a figure standing there.

A man.

He looked quite well built. Nothing too distinctive about him.

He had dark hair.

Wearing a cream T-shirt and blue jeans.

And he was standing right there, normal as anything.

Hands around his mouth.

Screaming.

Aoife froze.

Her body went icy cold.

The man lowered his hands. And looked right at Aoife.

"What..." Aoife started.

And then, out of nowhere, the man turned and bolted off into the woods.

She knew she should report back. She knew she should be careful.

But then, Max...

Instinct took over.

She ran.

Ran, with Rex alongside her.

Ran further into the woods.

She could hear people following.

She could hear the commotion.

But she could still see that man.

She could still see that bastard who'd stood there screaming in the middle of the woods.

She could still see him, and she knew she had to catch him.

She knew she had to...

Something else.

Something behind.

Something that made her stomach turn.

Her skin crawl.

Another scream.

Another scream, right behind her.

Right at where the *back* of the group would be.

She stood there. Looked back. And suddenly she realised how alone she was. How vulnerable she was.

Suddenly she felt in danger.

In deep, deep danger.

She turned around.

The man had gone.

The screaming had stopped.

But she felt like she wasn't alone.

She could see movement in the trees.

She could hear whispers.

She could hear Rex whining, panting. Like he was scared.

She backtracked. Slowly. Keeping her eyes on the surrounding woods at all times.

Went to run back towards the group. Towards the screams.

Ran. Ran as quickly as she could. Ran for her goddamned life.

She never thought she'd admit this, but she just wanted to see somebody.

She just wanted to run into somebody.

She didn't want to be alone.

She didn't want to—

Out of nowhere, someone in front of her.

She jumped. Reached for her knife.

Then she saw it was Kathy.

"Aoife," she said. "What—what happened?"

"It's a trick," Aoife said.

"What?"

"The screaming. It—it wasn't one of ours. It was nobody wounded. It..."

She looked over at Vincent then and saw him standing there. Sweating. Shaking. Muttering under his breath.

"It's them. This is what they do. This is how they get you. I'm sorry. I'm sorry. I'm sorry."

And hearing him say those words, hearing him say sorry repeatedly... there was something wrong about this.

"What the fuck is this?" Aoife said.

"Aoife?"

But Aoife wasn't stopping.

She tensed her fists.

Walked over to Vincent. The rest of the group all scattered everywhere. Screams erupting all over the place now.

Men.

Women.

Kids, by the sounds of things.

She grabbed Vincent by the scruff of the neck. Felt him worming away.

"Tell us the truth," Aoife said.

"They're here. I'm sorry. This wasn't meant to happen. It was supposed to be different."

She punched him. Hard.

"Aoife!" Kathy shouted.

But Aoife stood there and stared down at Vincent, and in her bones, she knew something was wrong.

"Tell us the truth!" Aoife shouted. "Now!"

Vincent turned over.

Looked up at her, face splattered with mud. A little blood trickling from his nostril. And those big wide eyes peering up. "I wanted to help you. I—I wanted to. Please believe that. Please."

She looked down into his crying eyes, and for a moment, she believed him.

She pitied him.

And then she heard a scream.

Right behind her.

Rex barking by her side.
She spun around and saw it all so fast.
Kathy.
Standing there one second.
Then out of nowhere, someone grabbing her.
Dragging her off into the darkness.
"Kathy!" Aoife shouted. Lunging forward.
Then she felt it.
Someone grabbing her.
The pressure against her throat.
"Not so fast," a familiar voice said.
Then, darkness.

# CHAPTER TWENTY-TWO

Aoife felt the darkness surrounding her and had no idea where she was.

Only that she was afraid.

She couldn't deny it. She was very afraid.

It was pitch black. It'd all happened so fast. The running. The screaming. Seeing Kathy disappear into the woods right before her eyes. Vincent lying there on the ground, shaking, cursing under his breath.

Terrified.

And then something happened.

The darkness.

And then the struggling.

Trying to fight. Trying to get away.

Someone dragging her with immense force. Dragging her into the woods.

And then, as much as she hated to admit it, as much as it made her feel weak... she'd screamed.

And now she was walking. Her wrists were tied. Her ankles felt bound together, too, but not so much that she couldn't walk. The blister on her foot that she'd burst trying to flee stung like hell, so much so it made her limp and wince. She tried to run to the left, tried to break off to the right, but it was useless. Someone would always drag her back, walk her forward.

It was a man behind her, that she was certain of. Holding on to her. Arm around her throat. So tight that sometimes she felt like she might pass out. Hell, sometimes she wondered if she *was* passing out and drifting back to consciousness again but was just too oxygen-deprived to realise.

She stumbled on, and she knew there was something wrong about all of this. Of how it went down.

The man standing there in the middle of the woods. Screaming.

Chasing after him.

Hearing more screams.

Going back to Kathy.

Vincent...

And then this.

She tried to shuffle from side to side, and she remarked on how weird the whole thing was, too. Vincent told her and Kathy that these people had killed his family. That they were ruthless, and they would strike hard.

But this...

This felt different.

This felt like an ambush.

An ambush from a group very accustomed to the woods.

An ambush from a group who knew exactly what they were doing.

But not the violent assault on the community Aoife was expecting.

She was still alive, after all.

Why?

Aoife kept on walking, heart racing. And it struck her, suddenly, like a bolt from the blue. Rex. Rex had been beside her. He'd been beside her, and she had no idea what'd happened to him. She didn't even have a clue how long had passed since she'd been captured. It could be minutes; it could be hours. She'd been so caught up in the shock that she hadn't kept count.

She thought of Rex, and she knew she couldn't give up. She couldn't just lay down and accept defeat.

She had to do something.

She had to fight.

She went to drag her feet into the ground and stop when suddenly, she came to a halt.

She froze. Tried to walk, but the person holding her wouldn't let her move. She tried to shout, tried to swear, but there was a gag around her mouth.

She stood there, shaking. She had no idea where she was. Only that, for whatever reason, they'd stopped now. And that couldn't be good news.

Because it meant they were at wherever these people were taking her to.

It meant...

Suddenly, a glimmer of light.

Just a glimmer. Right at the top left of her blindfold.

But a big enough glimmer that she could see something.

She blinked. Tried to squint. Tried to dislodge it to get it out of place.

And the more she struggled, the more she started to see.

Outside somewhere.

Some kind of factory up ahead.

Some kind of...

And then suddenly, the darkness returned, and she felt a push against her back and fell to the ground.

She hit the ground with a thud. Smacked her nose against the earth. Lay there for a few seconds, knees grazed. But relieved that she was finally free of the clutches of anybody.

She had an opportunity. She had a chance.

She went to stand up and run when she felt another punch

against her back, and once again, she went tumbling to the ground.

She lay there. Turned around. She couldn't see much. But it felt like her blindfold had been dislodged a little again. She could see something. Light. Some kind of figure.

She turned and looked up when she saw them standing over her.

A man. Bulky. Quite well built.

Mean look on his face.

A look Aoife had seen on plenty of guys. Guys on nights out. Letchy creeps, mostly.

He stood over her, and she could see him looking at her like she was meat.

"Go on," he muttered. "Get up. Run, little rabbit. Run."

She looked up at him.

Clenched her fists.

And then she went to stand.

To run.

And right away, his hands landed on her back, and—

"Oh, Marty," a voice said.

The grip on Aoife's back loosened.

She stumbled around. That voice. She recognised that voice.

She looked around. Saw the man who'd been holding her—Marty—standing there, looking a lot more sheepish suddenly.

"She slipped away. I was just—"

"No excuses," the man said. "They're people, Marty. They're people. Just like you and me. Don't forget that. They're just... unfortunate. They're just unlucky. But we should be grateful for them. So grateful for them. At the end of the day, they've saved our lives."

Aoife stood there, and she realised she knew where she'd heard that voice before.

She knew exactly who this man was.

It was Vincent.

And he was looking right at her.

Sympathetic smile on his face.

"Come on," he said. "Let's get you inside. You've seen quite enough already."

Aoife tried to run away.

But before she could move, Vincent was on her.

And then Marty was on her.

And then the blindfold was over her eyes again, and she was surrounded by darkness.

# CHAPTER TWENTY-THREE

Christopher Parker watched Marty drag the woman called Aoife off into the distance, and he really did feel bad about this whole thing.

He wiped his nose. He could taste the blood running from it onto his lips. She'd punched him hard. Real good punch to her, he had to admit.

And as much as he despised her for it, could he blame her, really?

She'd seen through his lies. She'd seen through his act.

A little too late, sure. But still, she'd seen through it.

And for that, he kind of respected her.

Besides. She couldn't really be blamed for what she'd done.

He sighed as he looked over at the Factory. He called it a Factory; they all did. Seemed less intimidating that way. Less... well. What it actually was.

Because this wasn't easy. It wasn't what he *wanted* to do. It wasn't what *anyone* wanted to do.

But when a group the size of the estate group appeared out of nowhere, he couldn't just let them pass.

None of them could.

He saw them being dragged down the hill towards the Factory. Carefully, for the most part. Which was good. They were people, just like him, just like his people. And they deserved to be treated with decency and respect. They weren't animals. They weren't cattle. They were more than that.

And yet... at the same time, thinking of them as cattle in some way, that did make it easier to swallow what he had to do.

What they all had to do.

He tasted a sickliness in his mouth. The sickliness of guilt. Guilt about it all. About how he'd been forced down this path. About how his family had been forced down this path.

His name wasn't Vincent, for a start. It was Christopher. To the outsiders, he was Vincent. Poor Vincent died in service of his people. A necessary sacrifice, as guilty as Christopher felt about it.

And that's what all of this was about. Survival. If people didn't survive, if they didn't step up, then humanity was finished.

Because it was pretty darned clear nobody was out there. Nobody was coming to the rescue. Nobody was out there in the world waiting to swoop in and help. If they were, they would've done by now. No way would Britain be left to go to waste. Not like this.

They were alone in this world. And they had to find their own ways to survive.

They had to fend for themselves.

And if that meant doing what was required to live—to doing whatever was required to live—then that's what he had to do.

He thought back to Vincent and felt bad. He was a runaway. But in the end, he'd been useful. His body had left enough fear in these people to cause a stir. To get them moving.

A necessary sacrifice.

And absolutely not a waste.

He watched the first of this group being led into the Factory. Struggling from side to side like they were pigs who knew something bad was coming. It helped for him to think of them like animals sometimes. Because thinking of them as humans was just too painful. He loved animals, too. So thinking of them that way wasn't exactly *helpful.*

But it just made it all a tiny bit easier to swallow.

For want of a better term.

But thinking of them as animals brought with it its own problems. Namely, they should be treated like people. They weren't bad people at the end of the day. They were just unfortunate. Wrong place, wrong time.

And really, Christopher and his people owed them gratitude above anything else.

He thought about Mum.

Thought of her last words to him as she lay there dying.

He thought about what she'd requested him do.

What she'd requested his brothers to do.

All to keep them alive.

He remembered the backlash.

He remembered the violence.

He remembered—

The taste.

Salty tears.

Rich, bloody steak.

No.

He couldn't think like that.

He just couldn't.

He watched more of this group get cordoned into the Factory, one by one. Looked like there were twenty. It'd been a good morning's work. A good hunt.

And the best thing of all?

There were still plenty of them out there in the woods. Disoriented. Scared.

Christopher closed his burning eyes.

They had plenty of supplies to last them a long, long time.

He thought of Mum again.

Thought of the moment he'd pressed that knife into her thick, fleshy thigh.

Thought of the sound of sizzling as her flesh hit the stove.

The searing.

The smell of burning.

And how like normal meat it smelled.

He thought of the vomiting.

The guilt.

The shame.

And then he thought of the fact he was alive.

All his people were alive.

He thought of it all, and he knew he was doing the right thing.

Because this was survival.

And, like it or not, the future of humanity depended on the survival of the fittest.

And he and his people were the fittest.

Because they were the only ones pragmatic enough to realise they had to do whatever they had to in order to survive.

*Whatever* they had to.

He watched the woman called Aoife approach the door to the factory. Watched Marty drag her away as she tried to break to the left, to the right.

He watched her, and he tasted the blood from his nostril.

And the most sickening thought of all?

The thought that made him feel like a monster and filled him with shame?

In that instant, Christopher couldn't help wondering what she was going to taste like.

He guessed he'd find out soon.

They all would.

# CHAPTER TWENTY-FOUR

Aoife opened her eyes and saw nothing but darkness.

But this was a different kind of darkness to the one she was used to. No vague outlines. No sense of where the window was, where the edge of the bed was. Nothing.

She tried to lift her hands, but they were bound together and seemed stuck to her waist somehow. She tried to stand, but she felt weak, disoriented. All around, she could hear sounds. Metal clanging. The sound of people mumbling. Screaming? Struggling? She couldn't tell.

She just knew that she was in danger. Serious danger.

This felt worse than the worst frigging hangover imaginable.

How had she ended up here?

What had...

And then it came to her.

The woods.

Chasing that screaming man.

The knife to her neck.

Being walked God knows how far through the woods, through the trees, totally blindfolded.

And then seeing him.

Seeing Vincent of all people standing there, looking down at her.

Not with a look of happiness. Not with any superiority, or anything like that.

But with a genuine look of sadness. A genuine look of remorse.

And then she'd been blindfolded again and dragged inside some place and then thrown into a room and...

She couldn't remember the rest. Figured she must've passed out with the shock, with the exhaustion.

But she was awake now.

She was alive now.

And she needed to know what the fuck was going on.

What had happened to her people.

What had happened to Max.

What had happened to Rex.

She tried to stand again but stumbled forward. Her knees ached. It felt like she'd fallen over more times than she could count.

But as she crouched there, body writhing with pain, shaking everywhere, she knew she couldn't just accept her fate.

She had to pick herself the hell up.

She had to get the hell to her feet.

She had to get the hell out of whatever this was.

She strained to stand. Her legs ached. Her ankles were sore and swollen. And her wrists were tied so tight that it felt like her fingers might explode, heartbeat throbbing right at their tips.

She stood there. Teeth chattering. Not cold, though. Nowhere near cold. It was stifling in here. So unbearably hot she wondered if she'd been tossed into some kind of sauna.

She stood there in the darkness and edged forward.

There had to be a way out.

There had to be someplace she could go.

There had to be—

"It's no use, Aoife. I'm sorry."

She froze the moment she heard that voice.

Tried to say something back, but her mouth was tied.

"There's nowhere to go," he said. "I don't say that to torment you. I just say it to save you causing yourself any more unnecessary suffering. The sooner you accept that this is your fate... the easier this can be. For all of us."

She stood there a few seconds. Shaking. Heart racing.

And then, suddenly, light filled her eyes.

Well. It was hardly light. The room she was in was murky. The walls were tiled black and white and covered in dark brown grime. The grey concrete floor looked cold.

It wasn't a big room at all. In fact, it wasn't really a room at all. More like a pen, of sorts, with metal gates either side of her.

When she looked into those metal gates, she saw what looked like blankets on the floor. Flies buzzing around.

And then...

People.

They were in a different section to her. In fact, all things considered, it looked like she'd got off lightly compared to the rest of the people here, crammed into those weird little pens together.

They were blindfolded. Blindfolded like her. Bound at the wrists. At the ankles. Some of them up against the gates at the front of their pens. Others just lying there like they were accepting their fate.

"I'm sorry to have to show you like this," he said. "But I think it's only fair you have some sort of explanation. Some sort of understanding. Because... Well. I have some kind of misguided idea that you might be different from the rest."

Aoife looked around and saw the man crouched before her.

Vincent.

He looked at her with that pity on his face. There was no panic to him now. He looked totally with it.

And again... it was that look of pity in his eyes that really got Aoife.

"When I apologise," he said, rather quietly, as if he didn't want anyone else to hear. "I am sincere. I didn't want to end up in this position. Nobody wanted to end up in this position. But humanity's on the brink, Aoife. You've seen it for yourself."

She wanted to speak. She wanted to shout. She wanted to say so much to this bastard.

But she couldn't because of the gag around her mouth.

He looked down at the tiled floor. Sighed. "I should probably say my name isn't really Vincent. It's Christopher. Christopher Parker. And I apologise for the performance at your community. But there was really no other way."

Aoife's head throbbed. What the fuck was he talking about? This looked like some kind of ambush, sure. But what was his deal here? Why was she still alive? Why were all these people alive?

And why did it seem like his apologies were... strangely genuine?

"I should also probably explain that the safe haven I spoke of isn't real. I apologise for that, too."

Her stomach sank. Not that she was surprised. But to hear it out loud... proof of Christopher's betrayal... it stung.

"And the group in the woods. The one I told you of. The one I escaped. They aren't real, either. So I suppose that's something."

That threw Aoife a little. If the group in the woods wasn't real, then who was he? And who were his people?

"What we've built here," he said. "What we do here. We do it to protect our people. To protect humanity. We do it because we have no other choice. It's not the easiest thing to do. But it's the only thing we can do. And you'll understand. In time, you'll understand."

He looked over his shoulder. Aoife could hear some movement, just out of view.

He looked back at her, then. "Anyway. Before I continue...

there's someone here. Someone I wanted you to see. Just to prove that we aren't savages. We're willing to communicate. If it's in all our best interests."

Aoife's chest tightened. She frowned. Who the hell was here to see her? What was he talking about?

He stood up, stepped aside.

And out of the darkness, Aoife saw a man being led into the pen.

A man being gently nudged towards her.

Blindfolded at first.

But then the blindfold was dragged away, and she looked into his eyes, and for a moment, through all this horror, she felt safe again.

Max.

# CHAPTER TWENTY-FIVE

Max saw Aoife before him, and for the first time in what felt like fucking forever, he actually felt something like hope.

But at the same time, he felt something like sadness, too. Because seeing her here. Seeing she'd been captured, too. Seeing that she'd been brought to this place... it made him feel uneasy. Sick to the stomach.

Because it meant she was trapped, just like him.

He felt the binds around his wrists. The way his arms were tied to his body, now. The way his ankles were chained together. And he saw Aoife sitting there, topless but for her underwear. Dehumanised, just like everyone else in this place.

The stench of sweat, shit, and piss. So strong.

And the bloke in front of him. A bloke he hadn't seen before. But who looked at him with a sort of sympathy that Max hated. He hated being fucking *pitied*. He'd punch the guys lights out if he got a chance. See who the fuck was pitying who then.

"I thought you two might want to see each other," the man said. "I believe this is the man you were looking for, right, Aoife?"

The sleazy fucker knew her name. Max wanted to put him in

his place. But he couldn't even speak for the gag around his mouth.

Because seeing her. Seeing her again, seeing her alive, especially after the last conversation they'd had in the woods. He wanted to apologise to her. Wanted to tell her how sorry he was for doubting her.

He wanted to hold her.

The man sighed. Looked at Max with that weird look of pity once more. "I know it's not ideal. Max here has been here a little longer than you have. In an ideal world, we wouldn't put you through this. But our resources are limited. That's the problem. It's not like we can freeze anything. So we do what we can to help. To look after you. To feed you. But maybe... maybe you two can be different."

Max had a feeling he knew what this bastard was talking about. But he didn't want to think it. He didn't even want to entertain the possibility that his gut feeling about what this place was—about what went on here—might actually be for real.

"I'd like the two of you to join me," the man said.

"Christopher?" one of the other guards—a woman with red hair—said.

"It's okay, Cassandra. Really. I think... Something deep down tells me these two might be able to offer more than most. There's something about them. And at the end of the day... we were all in their shoes once upon a time, right? We all had to be convinced. We all had to... see the way, so to speak."

Max looked over at Aoife, and he wanted to go over to her. To hold her. To protect her. That deep instinctive urge to look after her. She looked like hell. She always looked gorgeous, this natural radiance about her. But she hadn't looked healthy for a while, not surprising after all the drinking she'd been doing lately. But right now, she looked gaunt, and she looked pale, and she looked lonely, and she looked afraid.

And it pained him. Because he cared about this girl.

"Come on," Christopher said. He was a tall guy, messy brown hair, with these really goggly eyes that looked like they might just pop out of his skull at any second. "Let's get you both out of here. I think it's about time you see what we do here. So you can begin to understand."

He eased Aoife to her feet. Gently moved her forward. And he reached for the blindfold, over her head. "Don't worry. It's just for your own protection."

Max looked into Aoife's eyes, deep into them, and he wanted to say so much to her.

So much in just a glance.

And then the blindfold slipped from her eyes, and then the darkness covered his eyes, and once again, he saw nothing.

He felt himself being turned around. Then walking along. Walking along the corridor he'd already walked down. He could hear more mumbling. More muffled cries. He could smell shit and sick, and all of it was so grim, so horrible.

He wanted to make a break for it. Wanted to run.

But he knew there was no chance.

He felt a slight nudge against his back. And he wanted to believe it was Aoife, right there with him. Right there behind him. He wanted to believe that she didn't feel alone in this. That he was there for her.

He kept on going on this dark pathway to whatever the fuck he was going to find. Down some steps. Heard the bloke, Christopher, speaking to a few people, but they always said things he couldn't get his head round. Couldn't properly understand.

He felt himself being turned. Heard a door opening.

And then footsteps echoing before him.

He felt himself stop.

And then, for a moment, everything was quiet, and he wondered if he was alone. If there might be a chance.

Then, his blindfold fell away.

Light. Bright light. No idea how it was running in this place.

But it was there, and it was bright, and it was burning Max's eyes out.

He saw Christopher standing before him.

And then he saw something else, and his stomach turned.

His worst fears were realised.

"I'm sorry for this," Christopher said. "But it's about time you understood what's happening here. You two deserve to know."

When Max saw what was before him, he wished he was back under the safety of his blindfold again.

## CHAPTER TWENTY-SIX

When Aoife's blindfold lifted, she wasn't exactly sure what she was looking at, at first.

The room she was in was bright. Really bright. A white light beamed down above, flickering away. The fact there was light at all was something to behold in a powerless world. It looked like a lamp, so they must've got lucky. Flies swarmed around it, the sound of them filling the air with a discomforting hum. There was a strange smell in the air. Almost metallic. But mixed with something else, too. Kind of reminded her of trips to the butchers as a child. That strange smell of cold meat filling the air.

And that's when she realised why. Exactly why.

That's when it clicked.

There were meat hooks all around. But it didn't look like there were pigs hanging from them. Didn't look like skinned cattle were hanging from them.

It was quite clear that humans were hanging from them.

Skinned humans.

She looked around. Even if she had been able to say a word

through her gag, she wouldn't be able to anyway. She was frozen. Frozen to the spot.

All these meat hooks, people dangling down from them.

And then before her, what looked like a trough.

A trough filled with...

Blood.

And by the side of the trough, Christopher.

He stood there with a long, sharp blade in his hand.

Stared over at Aoife. That look of regret still present in his eyes.

"I'm sorry for you both to have to find out this way. It's... it's hard to process. Believe me, I know. But... but I figured if you could see how fast the process is. How easy we make it for people. How swift it is. Then maybe you'll begin to understand..."

He said more, but Aoife's attention drifted off. She couldn't get away from the scene before her. From what she was seeing.

The horror of it all.

And the scariest thing of all?

How apologetic Christopher seemed.

How *sincere* he seemed.

"I never intended things to go this way," he said. "In the early days... I was resistant. We all were. But in the end, I figured what better way to prolong humanity's survival than to use the greatest, most easily available resource of all? Hope."

Aoife tasted vomit in her mouth. She wanted to throw up.

"I'm not proud of what we do," Christopher said. And the way he looked at the floor, she actually believed him. He wasn't the sort of cannibal you usually saw in a post-apocalyptic movie. He was just so... normal. Unassuming.

And again. That's what scared her most.

"I'm not proud," he continued. "But we have a large group here. Just over twenty of us. And we're getting bigger. We're adding resourceful people to our group. People like—people like you. And maybe in time, when we get large enough, we won't need to do this. Maybe, in time when things get easier, we can find another way. But right now... We use the best resources available. And regretfully, the easiest resource to capture is humans themselves."

Aoife felt dizzy. She stumbled to one side. Hearing these words. Hearing the regret with which he spoke. And then the dissonance of seeing the blade in his hand...

She wanted to get away.

She wanted to run.

She wanted to—

"Cassandra?" he said. "Bring him out."

Aoife frowned. She saw movement over to the left. Saw struggling.

And then she saw someone walking to the middle of the room.

He was blindfolded. And he wasn't struggling much.

But she could see who it was, even with that blindfold on.

Amir.

She saw the woman with the red hair dragging him along, leading him to the middle of the room.

And then she saw something else. The plugs, deep in his eardrums.

She saw him be turned on the spot.

Watched the woman push him to his knees.

Saw him leaning over that trough.

"He can't hear," Christopher said. "He doesn't even know. That's the best way."

And then, out of nowhere, before Aoife could even process a thing, Christopher pressed the blade to Amir's throat.

Sliced it. Fast.

Amir struggled. He gargled out of the hole in his neck, which blood flooded out of, thick red.

"It's almost over," Christopher said, shaking his head. "I'm sorry. It's almost over. But you're doing a great thing. A great sacrifice."

Aoife watched Amir twitch from side to side.

Watched his body shake.

And then, after a painfully long minute, he slumped to his side.

She could only stand there.

She could only watch as two more people arrived in butcher's outfits and carted Amir away.

As they took him out of the room, to somewhere else.

She looked at his blood in the trough.

Looked at the area where he'd knelt.

Looked at the blade and at Christopher, who looked back at her.

Tears in his eyes.

"This man was strong. But he refused to cooperate. So this was his only fate. We need to talk about what path you two want to take. Very, very soon."

# CHAPTER TWENTY-SEVEN

Aoife sat against the wall and tried to scrub what she'd just witnessed out of her mind.

She was in a small room. Max was opposite her. They both had their gags off, now. Their blindfolds off. Still had the ties around their wrists, their ankles.

But Aoife hadn't been able to say a word to Max. Neither of them had been able to say a word to each other.

She could barely even look at Max.

All she had imprinted in her mind was Amir.

Being led out of that room, walking over to the trough.

Kneeling before it.

And then having his throat cut.

She kept on seeing him struggling. She couldn't unsee the stream of blood pooling out of his neck, more blood than she could ever imagine. And she couldn't unhear those gargling sounds he made. Like he was a pig in an abattoir.

And on top of that... Christopher.

Christopher, with his twisted logic that nothing else could be done.

And worse than that, his genuine sincerity. The apologetic tone, so at odds with the ruthless way he'd cut Amir's throat.

She saw Amir stumbling to the side of the trough, again and again.

Saw him being carried off, presumably for skinning, for gutting.

Only to be hung on a meat hook.

And then to be eaten.

She thought about her last interaction with Amir, and she felt terrible. He'd tried to speak with her. Tried to befriend her. Tried to connect with her when they were walking along in the woods, only for her to fire him off, again and again.

She remembered what Sam told her about him. How he'd been through his own struggles. His own losses. And how compelled she'd been to go speak to him, right in that moment.

But that moment was gone.

That opportunity was gone.

Amir was gone.

She felt a whole host of conflicting emotions. The group in the woods she'd run into in the night. It must've been these people. She'd warned Kathy. Told her something didn't seem right. But Kathy had insisted on evacuating everyone out of the estate anyway.

And really, Aoife knew they should have done more checks. They should have shown more scrutiny. But they were starving, and they had the chance of hope in the form of a safe haven from a mysterious stranger being promised. Couple that with the impending threat of destruction.

Could Aoife really blame Kathy, and everyone else, for acting in the way they did?

After all, if she felt so strongly about it, she still went along with it.

If she'd felt stronger about it, she could have stood up.

She could have done more.

And now, here they were. Facing certain death. Because there's no way they could possibly get on board with what Christopher was suggesting. There was no way they could allow that to happen.

"Amir was a good man," Max said.

Aoife's stomach sank the second she heard his voice. It was the first thing she'd heard from him since the entire ordeal in the slaughterhouse. A part of her wanted to speak to him. But a bigger part didn't want to hear it. Not right now.

Especially not about Amir.

"He was kind. Real hard grafter. And after what happened to his family..."

"What happened to his family?" Aoife asked.

She wasn't sure she wanted to know. Not right now. But she'd asked the question anyway, and she was bracing herself. Preparing.

Max sighed. "Hadn't been at the estate long when his mum got sick with the virus that was going round. He looked after her for ten days, right by her bedside, holding her hand. She died at the end of it. He didn't leave her side for three days."

Aoife felt the words like a punch to the gut.

"Three days later, his sister kills herself. Can't cope with the loss. Can't cope with this world. But still, he showed up to help build the gates, apparently. Even though people were begging him to take time off, he wanted to contribute. Said he wanted to keep on working in honour of his family. It's what they would've wanted."

Aoife went cold. Completely cold. Amir was a good guy. A good guy, and she'd turned him away. A good guy, and she'd had her head so far up her own arse that she hadn't even acknowledged his problems. She'd dismissed his pain.

And now he was gone. And she'd never have that opportunity, ever again.

"I could have been better," Aoife said.

"Yeah," Max said. "Yeah, you could."

She turned around to him. Saw him looking at his feet. He looked upset. She wasn't expecting him to speak like that. Not Max. She wanted him to be supportive.

But right now, he looked like he wasn't in that kind of mood.

"You were at the estate six months. Six whole months. And every day I went out, I heard stories of loss. Of suffering. But you know what? People just got on with things. They went through their suffering together. They let people in, and they contributed. But you just... you just bottled it all up. And *turned* to the bottle."

"Is now really the time?"

"If we want to survive, then now is exactly the fucking time, Aoife. Yeah."

He spoke with an anger she'd never heard from him before. And it got to her. Made her realise how out of touch she'd been.

And made her realise just how wrong she'd been going for so long.

"Survive?" Aoife said. "Does it look like we have much of a chance to you?"

"No," Max said. Bluntly. "But if we are to come up with a plan, it needs to be in the interest of all of us. Everyone here. We can't keep pushing people away. *You* can't keep pushing people away—"

"Just like you pushed everyone away?"

"I changed, Aoife. You... you changed me. And now you need to change, too. For yourself. And for everyone. Because I care. Only because I care."

She heard those words, and she felt a spark inside her. A spark when he said she'd changed him.

Because if she'd changed him and now she'd lost all hope... what hope was there for anyone?

"I don't know how we're going to do this," Max said. "But if we are going to do something, we need to work together. But that means you have to be with me. Fully with me. Do you understand?"

Aoife wanted to bite back. Wanted to admit defeat. She couldn't see a way out of this.

But then she took a deep breath, and she nodded.

"What's the plan?" she said.

Max nodded back at her. "I don't know how this plan ends," he said. "But I know how it starts."

She nodded again.

He looked around. Over at the door, where every now and then, Aoife heard footsteps.

Then he looked back at Aoife.

"It starts by us agreeing."

"Agreeing to what?"

"To... to Christopher's proposal. About joining him. About joining his people."

## CHAPTER TWENTY-EIGHT

The door to the room swung open, and Aoife knew right away she and Max had no more time to fuck around.

They had to act. Now. One way or another, they had to do something.

And as much as she hated the idea Max had suggested... she saw the logic in it. She saw the sense in it.

It might just be the only damned way they got out of this place.

She looked over at the grey metal door of this cramped, stuffy room they were in at the side of the main slaughterhouse, and she saw Christopher standing there. He had that sad smile to his dishevelled face, still. A sombre look about him. She swore he'd gone a shade greyer since she'd first set eyes on him, but she knew that was probably just in her head.

"I trust you've spoken amongst yourselves," he said as the metallic stench of blood wafted through into this small room. In the background somewhere, the sound of knives scraping against one another. She tasted vomit. Just hearing those knives scraping together... she knew what they were probably slicing apart. Knew what they were probably burrowing into.

People.

Amir.

"Well?" Christopher asked.

Aoife looked over at Max. She still felt torn about what he'd spoken of. Joining them? Joining these fuckers? These butchers?

But then, at the same time... what other choice did they have?

If they turned down their offer, they'd be thrown right back into their pens, and one day, they'd be dragged into that slaughterhouse and their throats would be sliced, and they wouldn't be able to do a thing about it.

Or they could play along. They could pretend they were on board.

They could buy themselves some time.

Some time that might not just save themselves but might save more of the people from the estate.

A responsibility Aoife didn't exactly want on her shoulders. But a responsibility she knew she was going to have to step the hell up and carry right now.

"Respectfully, we don't have all day here," Christopher said.

"We're... we're in," Aoife said.

Christopher looked over at her. And for a moment, for the first time in a long time, she swore she saw a genuine smile flicker across his face. Not a sad, sorrowful one. A genuine look of happiness. Of delight.

"Really?" he said.

Aoife looked at Max again, praying this was the right fucking call. "We... we figure we don't really have much of a choice. I can't... I can't pretend I'm on board with what you're saying. I can't stand here and pretend what you're saying sits right with me. It fucking repulses me. But maybe... I don't know. Maybe there's some logic to it. Some truth to it. Hard as it is to admit."

She felt sick even saying those words. Even lying about this was very fucking difficult. She didn't want to sound too enthusiastic, or he'd get suspicious. But she didn't want to seem too averse, either.

She had to be the closest thing to honest as she could—while lying through her teeth.

But she'd said them, now. And she just had to hope Christopher wasn't playing with them. Just had to hope he bought in to what they were saying.

"Good," Christopher said. Nodding. "Good. Then there's only one more step. A test. A regretful test, sure. But the only way of knowing whether the pair of you really mean what you're saying."

Aoife frowned. She didn't get it. Not at first. "What—"

"Follow me, please. Both of you."

She looked over at Max. She had a bad feeling about this. A really fucking bad feeling about this.

But she got up anyway. Max walked ahead of her, not saying a word. Not showing any kind of emotion.

Both of them followed Christopher out, back into the room where Amir's throat had been cut, and right there standing in front of the trough, Aoife saw a man.

She froze. Everything stood still. Time. Everything.

Because this man standing here...

It all happened so fast.

Christopher cut Max's wrist ties free.

Put a gag back over his mouth.

Then, Christopher placed the long blade into Max's hand.

Walked him over to the man.

Then placed Max right there, right behind him.

"Kill him," Christopher said. "Slit his throat. Then, I'll know you're truly ready."

# CHAPTER TWENTY-NINE

Max held the knife and looked down at the man kneeling over the blood-stained trough.

It was hot in here. Really bloody hot. The air reeked: sweat, shit, urine. Blood. His lips were chapped with the gag, back around his mouth now. He could hear the guy before him shivering. See the piss trickling onto the floor beneath him. Even though he was blindfolded, he was quite clearly aware of the situation. It wasn't the calm setup Christopher deluded himself about. Not one damned bit.

This guy before him was shaking, and he knew something was coming.

And still, that creep Christopher just stood by and watched.

No. *Worse*.

He wanted Max to kill this guy.

To prove his loyalty.

To prove he could step up to the plate with all the sick shit going down here, and to prove he was really on board.

To prove he could be trusted.

"Go on," Christopher said. "I would say take as much time as you need. I realise this isn't exactly the best situation to find yourselves in. And I realise it isn't easy. Not one bit. But time is of the essence here if we're to euthanise this man peacefully. We don't want him to be kept waiting. We don't want him to suffer. It wouldn't be fair."

Max heard these words, and there was so much he wanted to say. This was wrong. This was so fucking wrong. And it was the disconnect between what Christopher was saying and what he was being told to do that got him the most.

That calmness with which he spoke. Like he was genuinely remorseful about all this.

The actions and the things he was speaking about just didn't match.

Like he'd been totally desensitised.

"I'm sorry for how crude this is," Christopher said. "I don't want it to feel like I'm making you murder someone unnecessarily just to put you in an inescapable position. If you don't feel capable of doing this, that's completely fine, and it's understandable. But... but for want of not wanting to sound like I'm blackmailing you, you know what the other option is. The only other option."

And Max did. That was the thing. If he didn't step up here, if he didn't do the impossible, the unthinkable, then he'd be thrown back into that pen, and he'd be fucking meat in no time, as would everybody else here.

But if he did it... then maybe there'd still be a chance to get out of this place.

Maybe there'd be a way to save everyone else.

He looked at the man kneeling before him. At the birthmark on his neck. He heard his shaking breaths as he kneeled, right above that trough.

He held the knife in his hand. Clenched the blade. Tight.

Shaking.

He didn't want to do this.

He couldn't do this.

But then what choice did he have?

He looked over at Aoife. Her gaze was wide. All she looked at, all she saw, was this man. She was staring right at him. Looked frozen. Completely frozen.

Max wanted to look into her eyes. He wanted her to look back at him and for her to somehow convey to him that this was the right thing to do. It was the only thing they could do.

But he didn't get anything.

"Please, Max," Christopher said. "Please don't let this man suffer. He's comfortable now. But not for much longer. Not if you leave him like this. And his fate is sealed anyway. Please."

Max looked at Christopher. Saw the tears welling in his eyes. And he wanted to bury the knife into him. He wanted to bury it deep into this self-pitying fucker's throat.

But then he looked back at the man before him.

Saw him shaking. Shivering.

And then he inhaled, deeply.

Tried to push aside all outside thoughts. All the negative emotions that were creeping in.

Tried to use the old mind tricks he'd learned in the military.

The tricks about calmness. About composure.

He put the blade against the man's neck.

Heart racing.

He didn't want to do this.

He didn't want to do this, but he had to.

There was no other option.

There was no choice.

There was...

Then he heard something.

Right under the gag, he could just about hear the man speaking.

Muffled, but speaking.

"Please. I'm sorry. Please. Please..."

He felt the warmth of the man's body.

Felt the piss seeping onto his feet.

He felt him, and a wave of sadness came over him.

A wave of sorrow.

He couldn't do this.

He just couldn't do this.

He stepped back.

Threw the knife to the floor.

And then he turned around and walked away.

Christopher stood there. Watched, without saying a word. A real look of regret in his eyes.

"I understand," Christopher said. "I do get it. Really, I do. But now..."

It all happened so fast.

The sound of a struggle.

Max turned around.

Saw Aoife lunging for the knife.

And for a moment, he thought she might go for Christopher.

But it was too late. There were two more people, and they were onto her.

She wouldn't make it.

She wouldn't...

That's when it struck him.

She wasn't going for Christopher at all.

She grabbed the man kneeling over the trough by the hair.

Pressed the blade against his throat.

Muttered something to him.

And then, before Max or anyone could do a thing, she cut his throat.

# CHAPTER THIRTY

Aoife saw the man crouching over the trough and right away, she recognised him.

It might be dark and murky in here, other than that horrible bright artificial lamp shining down in the middle of the room. And he might be blindfolded. Gagged.

But she recognised him.

Recognised the shape of his body. The way the right side of his ribcage protruded just a little more than was natural.

She recognised the birthmark on the back of his neck.

And she recognised the way he shook when he was scared, too.

There was absolutely no doubt about it.

This man was her ex-husband.

This man was the man who'd broken her heart.

This man was Jason.

She stood there and watched as Max walked over to him. She couldn't take her eyes off Jason, not for a second. She could hear Christopher saying things, going through that self-pitying bullshit again and again and again.

But she didn't hear the content of his words. Not anymore.

She could only see Jason, kneeling there.

And she could only feel the conflicting emotions surging through her body.

Anger.

Anger towards him for what he'd done to her.

Anger towards him for being a sick, twisted pervert.

Anger towards him for making her feel like she wasn't strong enough to get over him, even after everything he'd done.

And there was something else, too. Flashes of memories that she couldn't force out of her mind even though they were tainted with the stains of what he'd done.

Covered with the sticky, greasy fingerprints of his sordid, twisted secrets.

The memories of being in the woods with him, camping, cooking sausages over a fire and ending up with food poisoning. Brutal and horrible at the time, but something they looked back on with such amusement. Such happiness.

Or the day he proposed in New York, on top of the Empire State Building. Cheesy as hell, and cliche as hell. Probably the ninetieth marriage proposal of the day up there.

But still, the sweetness of it. The happiness she'd felt.

The happiest moment of her life.

And then the other memory.

The dark memory, like a cloud above her.

A memory she tried to suppress.

A memory she fought against, even to this day.

A memory the drink suffocated.

Soon after she'd caught him masturbating over indecent images of children, and soon after she'd sworn she didn't want to see his face again, she'd started feeling sick in the morning. She'd started peeing a lot. Started feeling exhausted and snappy. Throw in a missed period, and the signs were looking pretty clear.

And as much as she tried to ignore the symptoms and the signals, she couldn't run away from them forever.

She remembered sitting in her bathroom, preparing to pee on that pregnancy test, and knowing already what the result was going to be. It was like God was fucking with her. Like he was throwing just one final spanner in the works. One final thing for her to deal with.

She couldn't keep it. She knew that. She couldn't look a kid in the eyes and know he was the offspring of that monster.

But at the same time... she didn't want to get rid of it. She wasn't anti-abortionist in a traditional sense. But she did feel a weird attachment towards a life, especially a life growing inside her. And she felt guilty about robbing that life of a chance.

In the end, nature acted anyway, made the decision for her. She miscarried at eleven weeks. Most painful two days of her life, and she'd been through a hell of a lot of pain.

She never did tell Jason about that. And the saddest part of it all? A part of her wanted to have that child because she knew it would maintain something of a thread between her and Jason.

Even after everything he'd done.

The very foundations of a toxic relationship, right?

She saw Max holding the blade to his neck, and she wanted him to do it. Wanted him to get it done. Wanted him to end it. To finish it.

She wanted him to find the strength inside him. He was strong. So strong. He could do this and spare Aoife the responsibility.

It all happened so quickly.

Max stepped away.

Tossed the knife to the floor.

Immediately, two people were on him.

She saw the knife.

Saw that nobody was looking at her.

And she remembered Max's words.

*We can't just stand by and let this happen. It's our only damned choice, Aoife.*

She heard those words spiralling her mind.

And then she lunged towards the knife.

She heard the shouting.

Heard the commotion.

And then, before anyone could register what was happening, she pressed the knife to Jason's throat.

She leaned towards his ear.

Heard him snivelling.

Crying.

And she knew she couldn't just say nothing.

She knew she couldn't let him get away that easily.

"I don't forgive you," she whispered. "And I never will."

And then she sliced Jason's throat.

Blood splattered over her hands and into the trough. Streams of it splashed back onto her face.

She watched Jason struggle. Watched him try to clutch his wheezing throat as he tried to stop the bleeding.

She watched as he passed out.

As he started twitching.

As more bubbles of blood foamed out of the dark wound across his neck.

And she watched as two men came and took him away.

She looked around at Christopher, then.

He stood there. Wide-eyed.

"Good," he said. Clearly struggling for words. "You did... you did good."

And then he looked around at Max. "Take him away. Aoife stays with me."

She watched the two men drag Max away.

She looked into his eyes, saw the horror of what she'd just done on his face.

But she looked right at him the whole time.

"Come on, Aoife," Christopher said. "Let's get you out of here."

She watched as Max disappeared behind his blindfold.

As he disappeared behind the door.

As the door slammed shut after him.

She was on her own now.

# CHAPTER THIRTY-ONE

Aoife stood in a quiet little room all on her own and had no idea what to expect next.

She had no concept of what time of day it was. It was always dark in here, it seemed. She didn't have a clue how long it'd been since she'd been captured and brought here, either. Could be one endless night, could be a week. She had no idea.

Outside, she could hear thunder. Heavy rain. It soothed her. A thunderstorm was always a relief in the stifling, stuffy heat of summer. The smell of petrichor, one of her favourite words. Hated the fact that Jason had taught her that word when they'd been holidaying in Dubrovnik after running through the streets of the old town to escape a torrential storm. Hated that she enjoyed the memory. That she was happy in the memory.

She thought of Jason and of what she'd just done to him, and she still couldn't quite believe it. It hadn't quite sunk in. That man. That man she'd cut the throat of, ruthlessly, was her ex-husband.

That man she'd loved once.

But that was before he'd broken her heart.

Before he'd shown his true colours.

His sick, twisted true colours.

She thought about the odds of it being him kneeling there, of all people. The chances of it being someone she detested so strongly. Someone who figured so strongly in her life. She didn't believe in fate, but that's what it felt like.

And she thought about how easily she'd cut his throat. How *right* it felt.

If it was anyone else kneeling there, would she have been able to do it?

She wasn't sure. She'd seen the way Max struggled. And Max wasn't exactly the kind of bloke you'd imagine struggling to do something like that in the name of saving the majority.

She'd done what she'd had to do. The only thing she could possibly do.

And she did not regret it for one moment.

If anything... she felt relieved.

She'd had a weight on her shoulders for so many years, and now Jason was gone, that weight was gone too.

She stood in this quiet room. The walls were tiled white. There were brown stains on there. Stains that were presumably from the blood of so many others. A nasty stench in the air, like raw meat of a side-street butchers, clinging to her nostrils as she breathed. That taste of vomit in her mouth and that constant feeling of anxiety in her stomach.

She wondered where things went from here. How much further was she going to have to go to appease these people?

And how the hell was she going to save people from this place?

Just how deep would she have to go?

Just how far would she have to fall?

But she was here, and the very fact that she was here meant she had an opportunity. She had a chance. Max hadn't been afforded that chance. He'd been taken away. He hadn't proven himself to Christopher.

So now it was all on Aoife.

Now, it was all in her hands.

She knew, as she stood here, all on her own, that everything Max told her earlier was right. That she'd chosen a convenient fucking time to start caring.

But it wasn't because she didn't care. Quite the opposite. She was *afraid* of caring.

She'd cared so many times already and lost so many times already that the thought of caring and losing all over again just filled her with dread.

But as she stood there, shivering, so many lives depending on her, she knew she had to step the fuck up.

She had to fight out of this place and save as many of the people from the estate—and as many people as possible.

It was her duty.

It was her responsibility.

And she'd die trying.

She took a long, deep breath, that meaty stench in the air still hanging in her nostrils.

And she prepared for whatever was heading her way.

But one thing was for sure.

She was getting out of this place.

She was getting the hell out of this place, and she was—

The door beside her opened.

Christopher stood there. Half-smile on his face.

"It's time," he said.

Aoife frowned. "Time for what?"

"To see just how serious you are."

# CHAPTER THIRTY-TWO

Aoife followed Christopher down a long, endless corridor, blindfolded once more, and wondered what the fuck she was going to find at the end of it this time.

The darkness was growing more and more disorienting. The torrential rain outside, hammering down, fell heavier and heavier. Thunder exploded like the heavens were battling with one another. Like there was a war out there.

Again, Aoife found the calm in that thunder. She found comfort and solace in the storm. Always been the way, weird as it may sound. Went right back to childhood. Camping in the woods with Dad. Heavy rain. Sitting with a sugary cup of hot chocolate from his flask, always so sweet. Staring out at the rain as it fell from the sky, trickled down the leaves.

She followed Christopher through the darkness. Smelled that horrible stench in the air. The stench that so many of them living here must be desensitised to. Must be acclimatised to.

"Mind the step," Christopher said. "We're heading outside."

Aoife frowned. This was new. She didn't know where she was going. Was outside good news or bad news? She wasn't sure.

She felt around with her foot for a step, then descended

slightly. Felt the stones grind underneath her foot. Felt cold rain falling heavily from above, soaking her sweat-drenched hair. She smelled the fresh air in the cool breeze. She had no idea how long she'd been stuck inside. Probably wasn't as long as she thought in all truth. But it felt like forever.

And now she was outside, she felt a glimmer of hope.

She was outside. Which meant there was a chance. A chance to get away. A chance to make a break for it. A chance to escape to the woods and start a new life. Alone.

Max would want that if the odds seemed impossible, right?

But then she felt that tug in the opposite direction. The sense of responsibility she had.

She was the only one who could help the people trapped here. She was the only one who could save them.

She couldn't abandon them. She couldn't just leave them behind.

She felt the rain hammering down. Saw a flash somewhere, beyond the sight of her blindfold.

And then she felt a soft hand against her back. A hand that made her skin crawl.

"Come on," Christopher said. "It's just through here. A little step again."

She gritted her teeth. Wanted to tell him to fuck the hell off and get his hand off her.

But at the same time, hard as it was, she knew she had to keep on playing the game.

She felt solid floor underneath her feet. Like wood.

Smelled something in the air. Like a barbecue.

Like something cooking.

Meat.

She felt Christopher stop her. The rain had stopped falling on her now. But she could still feel the wind.

And then suddenly, out of nowhere, her blindfold was

removed, and her gag was removed, and she could see and breathe.

She was under some kind of tarpaulin. Looked like some sort of outdoor dining area with wooden tables. People gathered around them, looking at her. Watching closely.

The first thing that struck Aoife was that these people didn't look stereotypically "evil" or anything like that. Sure, they didn't exactly look friendly. Didn't exactly look the most welcoming and trusting of a stranger. But she couldn't really blame anyone for that. She was exactly the same on that front, surely.

But they looked... normal.

Ordinary.

There was a plate of food on a table before her.

And seeing it made her salivate.

She was so hungry. Hadn't eaten in what felt like forever. She could feel the juices in her mouth kicking in. She could taste it, that juicy steak. The fat dripping from it. The smell of it...

And then her stomach turned.

Christopher walked over to it. Picked it up.

And then he walked over to Aoife.

That self-pitying look on his face, once more.

And as he held it out to her, Aoife's stomach dropped even more.

The taste of stomach acid crept up her throat, into her mouth. She felt dizzy, but she couldn't let any of the onlookers see she was fazed. She had to stay calm. She had to keep her composure. Had to keep her control.

Because she knew what this was.

"It's a kind of tradition we have," Christopher said. "After a great sacrifice. It's only fair that the one who made the sacrifice should be the first to eat. As a mark of respect for the one who lost their life. And as a sort of... self-punishment, I suppose."

Aoife stared at this steaming piece of steak before her, and she felt like she was going to vomit, there and then.

Because this was Jason.

This was a piece of Jason, right before her.

"Go on," Christopher said, staring at her. The rest of the eyes under this tarpaulin staring at her. Watching. Waiting. "I don't mean for this to be a test, either. But it is, I suppose. You have to be willing to do the horrible. The unthinkable. It's the only way, Aoife. You've done so well already. But it's the only way."

She looked at that plate of meat before her.

Looked at that slab of it.

Looked at how it was cooked.

Medium rare.

Just how she liked her steak.

Looked at the little trickle of blood coming from underneath it.

She thought of Max.

Thought of what he told her.

About how far they were going to have to go to help the people here.

And how she was the only one who could help, now.

She closed her eyes.

"I know it's not easy," Christopher said. "It's never easy. But—"

She snatched the plate from his hand.

Grabbed the piece of meat.

The piece of Jason.

*Whatever she had to do.*

*Whatever she had to do.*

She didn't think about the meat as she put it in her mouth.

As she chewed down on it.

She didn't think of it as...

As him.

She just thought of the lives she was saving.

Thought of the people from the estate.

Thought of Max as she chewed and she swallowed and she tasted blood and...

She opened her eyes.

Saw the people looking up at her.

Saw Christopher looking at her. Smiling, too.

"That wasn't the flesh of sacrifice," he said. "It was one of the last pieces of sheep meat we had here. But we had to know. We just had to know how willing you were. And now we do... now we know you're willing... you're one step closer to being one of us."

A combination of sickness.

Of relief.

Christopher took her back to a room. Sat her down in there, gagged.

He looked down at her as he stood by the door.

"You're doing well. Really. What you've done, how quickly you've adapted... it's not easy, I know. But it'll all be over soon. I promise."

He smiled at her.

Then he closed the door and disappeared.

She sat there, in the darkness, on her own.

Shaking.

Crying.

She waited until she was absolutely sure Christopher was gone before vomiting into her gag.

# CHAPTER THIRTY-THREE

Christopher walked away from Aoife's room and couldn't help wondering if everything was too good to be true.

It was late, and he was exhausted. He needed to sleep. It'd been a long day today. A successful day, too. They'd captured twenty-three in total, and that would give them enough food to last them a long time. Just had to keep them alive and keep them healthy for as long as possible. Keep them muscular, lean. Not too fatty.

And then there were the others. The ones who'd slipped away in the woods. Who'd likely returned to the "safety" of their home, back at the estate.

If Christopher could capture those... they'd really be in a good position to see themselves through the rest of the year.

He felt optimistic about the thought. Sick, sure. But optimistic. At the end of the day, there were mouths to feed here, and this was the best way to feed them. He didn't like what he did. He battled with the morals and the ethics of what he did every single day.

But in one hundred years, when humanity was still standing

and the power had returned, people would look back on him as the man who had saved this nation.

And the methods of which he'd achieved that?

They'd be merely a footnote.

But as he walked down the corridor of the Factory and headed back towards camp, it was Aoife he thought of. She was surprising. Truth be told, he hadn't really had any expectations for her initially. Thought she was tough and might come in handy. Same with Max.

But the way she'd shown willingness. Not just to slaughter, but to *eat*...

It seemed too good to be true.

It felt too good to be true.

And that's what bothered Christopher.

What if it *was* too good to be true?

He shook his head. He'd always been a paranoid guy. Mum used to say as much. *Give him enough time alone in a dark room, and he'll be convinced the walls are conspiring against him*. He wasn't sure why it was. Probably because he wasn't the most popular kid at school. He wasn't particularly weird or anything like that. Him and his siblings had just been pretty poor. They weren't the cleverest, but they were kind of nerdy at the same time. Which didn't make them the most popular.

They were of a similar age. Well, Peter was his twin brother, so exactly the same age in his case. But mostly, they stuck together. They were close. Always close. Which made how it ended even more of a shame.

Christopher stopped when he thought of that day.

Shuddered.

The memories.

Too hard to stop now.

Coming at him too fast that he couldn't do a thing to prevent them from racing towards him.

The memory of Mum.

Of honouring her wish.

*Eat me. Be resourceful. Honour me by eating me...*

The arguments his brothers and him had over it.

The debates.

Peter grabbing Christopher when he tried to slice into her flesh and...

Christopher closed his eyes.

Shook his head.

He didn't want to think about that. Didn't want to go there.

But there was no holding it back. No repressing horror like that.

The horror of murdering his brothers.

The horror of feeding on their flesh.

On his mother's flesh.

And then the horror of realising that might just be the most viable solution of all.

For everyone.

He thought back to the first day he'd run into someone like-minded about the whole thing. And how rapidly it progressed from there. How their numbers grew. And how people who were initially reluctant were soon on board when they realised just how much *easier* it was to catch a human than it was to catch an animal. And how much further human flesh went than pretty much any other readily available animal.

People didn't have to like it. Christopher didn't *like* it.

He just knew it was the best way. The easiest way.

And sure, he'd be judged in the afterlife if the afterlife was even a thing.

But he intended to prolong his time in this life for a good lot longer just yet.

"She's good," a voice said.

Christopher looked around. Saw Cassandra standing there. Cassandra was tall. Long ginger hair. Deathly pale skin covered in tattoos. She was one of Christopher's most reliable friends.

One of the most loyal people here. He trusted her with everything.

"I sense some hesitation in your voice," Christopher said.

Cassandra sighed, walking alongside Christopher. "It's not that I'm hesitant. It's just that I'm a little... well."

"Well what?"

"Alarmed, maybe?"

"In what way?"

Cassandra shook her head. "It's hard to explain. None of us *want* to do what we're doing here. Well, other than maybe Ken, but Ken's a fuckin' weirdo anyway. But like, none of us really want this shit. But the way she killed that bloke. And the way she ate that meat. Almost as if she's..."

"Trying to prove something," Christopher said.

Cassandra nodded. "Exactly."

Christopher looked back at the Factory. The storm was wild. Rain hammered down from above. The wind battered him, and flashes of lightning blasted to the earth.

"I don't know what else to do to," Christopher said. "That's my only problem here. She's shown great loyalty and... enthusiasm, for want of a better word. What else are we supposed to do about her? To find out how loyal she is?"

It was right then that Cassandra did this smile that Christopher hated. 'Cause it was creepy. Almost like she got a kick from all this. Not something he was keen on. But then she was a bit of a weirdo, and it wouldn't surprise him if she were the type who liked snuff movies and shit like that back in the old world.

She walked right up to him. Looked right into his eyes as rain pounded down on the roof above.

"I think I know *exactly* how we find out how loyal she is. Once and for all."

# CHAPTER THIRTY-FOUR

Max sat in the darkness, but the room was filled with visions of everything that had happened.

Holding that blade to the man's throat. Hearing him begging for his life. Smelling the shitty stench rising up into the air and feeling the warmth of the piss as he emptied his bladder in fear.

He'd stood there with that blade, shaking, and he knew damned well if he was serious about his plan of getting out of here that he was gonna have to do something nasty. Really fucking nasty.

But then...

He hadn't been able to. No way could he go through with that.

Dropping the knife. Feeling that sense of defeat. Knowing damned well there was no fucking chance any of them were getting out of this mess now.

And then, out of nowhere, Aoife.

Grabbing the knife.

Slicing that guy's throat.

He kept on seeing it, again and again, flashing across his mind's eye. Made his skin crawl, truth be told. 'Cause as much as he knew Aoife could be tough... that was just goddamned ruthless.

And he wasn't sure how it made him feel. Sacrificing an innocent man to save the rest of the people? Hell, he'd been in positions like that before in life. In the military. Even in the police. It's all about weighing up the pros and cons of any given situation and figuring out which might be the least tragic.

But it was one thing to *know* that theoretically and then another to fucking *do* it.

He shook his head. Pushed those thoughts away. Whatever Aoife was doing, at least he knew she was trying. At least he knew her head was in the game.

At least he knew she was finally on board with trying to help people. To save people.

He just hoped she didn't lose herself any more than she already had.

It was pitch black. He could hear thunder outside. He felt cold, even though he knew damned well it was stuffy and warm in here. Constantly stunk of shit and piss. Something he was just growing used to now—if anyone could ever grow used to it.

He sat there, and he felt useless. Really fucking useless. He'd suggested an escape plan to Aoife. Suggested playing along with their way of doing things here. And now it was all on her. Now, it was in her control. In her hands.

He wasn't sure how he felt about that. Never liked shit being out of his hands. Preferred being in the driver's seat, so to speak.

But then he paused. Took a breath.

Aoife might've lost her way these last few months. But she was strong. And she was intelligent. And she was fierce.

She'd find a way out of this, one way or another.

She'd think of something.

And she'd die trying if that's what it came to.

His jaw tensed.

The thought of losing Aoife, too...

He didn't want that to be on him. Not after Kathryn. Not after David.

Not with the way he felt about her.

He thought of Aoife without meaning to now. He felt conflicted about her. Part of him saw her as a daughter. Another part of him...

There was something more than that.

Something closer.

A warmth.

A connection.

He shook his head. Now really wasn't the fucking time to be thinking about a romance with her, was it?

But if ever he did get out of here...

He shuffled against the wall when he felt something in the palm of his hand.

Something wooden. Hard to make out what it was at first.

Then it clicked.

The wooden boat. The one he'd made for Aoife.

It was here.

So if it was here... she must've put it here, somehow.

And if she'd put it here...

Was that a sign?

Was there a way out he didn't know about?

A way of escaping this place she was trying to point him towards?

He searched the floor. Searched every tile with his hands and fingertips. Desperately searched every inch of it, only to be met with nothing.

He slumped back against the wall. Heart racing. Sweating. Maybe she'd just put it there for moral support. To show she was still here. That she was working on something.

Or maybe she'd just dropped it.

Hell. Maybe it wasn't even the wooden boat at all. Maybe he was losing his damned mind in here. Maybe it was just a chunk of wood. He didn't know. Didn't have a goddamned clue.

He went to sit back when he heard footsteps.

The rattling of keys.

He sat up.

Heart beating faster.

Aoife?

Could it be her?

Could she be here for him?

He heard the footsteps stop, right up ahead of him.

A silence. A tense damned silence that felt like it lasted forever.

And then, finally, someone spoke.

"Max," Christopher said. "I'd like you to come with me. We've got something we'd like you to... to be a part of."

## CHAPTER THIRTY-FIVE

It all happened so fast.

Aoife was sitting there in her dark room. No clue how long she'd been in there. No clue whether she'd slept. No clue about anything at all.

And then, out of nowhere, there was a huge bang, and someone was holding her by the armpits, dragging her out of the room.

She couldn't see anything, but she could sense right away this wasn't Christopher. They were harder on her. Held her armpits a little tighter than Christopher did, less sensitively. Sharp fingernails buried into her skin.

Aoife wasn't sure why, but she was pretty sure this was a woman.

She felt the woman pushing her along. Not saying a word to her. Just pushing her along, much less sensitively than Christopher did. Much less patiently. She had no idea where she was taking her. No idea where she was leading her.

But then, out of nowhere, they came to a stop. Aoife banged her head against something, hard.

And then next thing she knew, her blindfold was off her, and she was looking into the eyes of a woman.

She'd seen this woman before. A few times. She was there at the camp when she'd eaten the meat. And she was there when Aoife had killed Jason, too. She was a red-haired woman with ghostly pale skin. And she had this weird, sinister look about her. Definitely the most sinister-looking cannibal in this place, as absurd as that statement sounded.

She held Aoife by her throat. Tight.

"Listen," she said. "I don't know what your game is. I don't know what your deal is. But... but Christopher likes you. He sees something in you. I don't know what. I mean, I guess you're okay. I guess you're kinda pretty. But no matter what happens, you need to know your place, okay?"

Aoife gargled. Strained to break free of this woman's grasp. What the fuck was her deal?

The woman leaned in closer to Aoife's face. Her breath stunk of tooth decay. Aoife knew what tooth decay smelled like 'cause Dad had a run-in with it once. That's the main thing she remembered about it. The smell, bittersweet, like something rotting, turning sour. Knowing when he'd been in the bathroom. Knowing when he'd been *anywhere.*

That goddamned stench, recognisable everywhere.

"I don't know what you'll do next," the woman said. Almost like she was speaking to herself more than Aoife. "Honestly, I want to think you'll crumble. But... but I really don't know. Kind of scares me. Kind of interests me. We'll soon see. But if you do go the road Christopher wants you to... just you remember I've got a close fucking eye on you, okay? At all fucking times."

Aoife went dizzy.

She gasped to breathe.

She was going to pass out.

She was going to collapse.

She was—

The woman loosened her grip.

Let her drop to the floor.

"Now come on," she said. "No time to waste. Let's see how you get on with the next stage."

Before Aoife could even catch her breath, she was on her feet again. Being pushed down the corridors of this abattoir. Only her blindfold hadn't been put back on. So she could see the scenes around her.

The people, blindfolded, crammed into these pens.

Half-naked.

Shaking.

Scared.

She looked all around, and the horror hit her again when she saw the meat hooks. When she saw the bodies dangling from them. Flies swarmed across one up on the left, something Aoife found disgusting, but that this woman didn't seem too fazed by.

She looked beyond the meat hook at the next pen and saw something that made her stomach turn.

Sam. Kathy. From the estate.

They were in that pen together.

Both of them blindfolded.

Naked but for their underwear.

And both of them looking like they'd already given up.

She saw them both, and she felt a surge of sadness. And a wave of helplessness. But mostly just guilt. Because these were good people. They were good people, and she should have stood up more when they'd decided to leave for the safe haven. She should have been more honest about the trepidation she felt.

"I'll make things right," she whispered. "I promise I'll make things right."

She looked around and saw a rusty metal door in front of her.

A door with a window in it.

And outside, bright light.

Bright, summer light.

She felt the nerves kick in, then. Because as much as it looked nice out there... there was an ominous feeling about all of this.

Where was Christopher?

What was happening here?

And why was there no sign of Max anywhere?

She reached the door. The woman reached for the handle, went to open it.

And before she could, she leaned right into Aoife's ear.

"I hope you're ready for this, hun. Really. For your sake."

She pecked her on the cheek, that nasty breath clouding around her again.

And then she opened the door.

Pushed Aoife outside.

Aoife squinted. The light was so bright, and it felt like a long time since she'd seen any.

There was a sandy area up ahead. Right before the covered areas she'd eaten in last night—or whenever the hell that was. Must've walked right across this area yesterday.

People were standing around. About eight of them. Men and women. Looking at her with curious eyes. Watching closely.

But it was in the middle of the scene that Aoife's attention went.

When she realised exactly what she was looking at, her stomach turned, and her body went cold.

Christopher was standing right there, right opposite her.

He looked at her with a half-smile. Nodded.

Knife in hand.

"I'm sorry for this," he said. "But we need to be absolutely sure. And this is the only way, Aoife. It's the only way."

She saw the man kneeling by his side.

Naked.

She watched Christopher lift the sack away from his head.

And then she saw his face.

Saw his squinting eyes.

Saw him looking around everywhere.

He looked up at Aoife, and Aoife looked back at him, and suddenly, she knew exactly what this was.

Christopher walked over to her.

Held the knife out to her.

"I'm afraid we require one final show of loyalty," he said. "That's all we want from you. I know this isn't easy. But you know what you have to do."

She looked across at the man kneeling opposite her, and her stomach sank even further.

It was Max.

## CHAPTER THIRTY-SIX

Aoife saw Max kneeling on the ground before her, and she wasn't sure how they were going to get out of this one.

He was on his knees. The sun shone down brightly, so bright it gave her a headache right away. He was covered in sweat. And he didn't have a blindfold on anymore. He didn't have a gag over his mouth, either. She could see the red marks where the gag had been tied around his mouth, sore edges to his lips. She could see the way he was looking up at her, with tired, exhausted eyes. She could see so, so much.

And yet, it was the knowledge of what she was being made to do here that filled her with the most fear. With the most dread.

Christopher held out the knife before her. "I know it's not ideal. It's not what any of us want. Nobody wants to see anybody die. Particularly not someone you're clearly close to. But I... I see something in you, Aoife. I think you're strong. Like us. You need to step over the hurdle. You need to make a sacrifice. To prove your loyalty. We all have. I... I have. More than most."

She looked at Christopher, then back at Max. She was shaking all over. This fucker actually thought she was going to kill Max?

He actually thought she was going to murder him in cold blood, right here? Just to prove her "loyalty"?

And the rest of these people. All standing by. All watching. All waiting. None of them looked like they were enjoying it, aside from the woman who'd threatened her before. She looked like the only one here who was getting any sort of kick out of this.

"Aoife," Max muttered.

She looked around at him. Saw him kneeling there. Staring back at her. And she could see that look in his eyes. She knew what that look was. And it tore her apart.

Because that was a look like he was trying to communicate something with her.

She didn't want to think what he might be trying to say to her.

Because deep down, she already knew.

"I... I can't do this," Aoife said.

Christopher scratched at the back of his hand. "I understand it's tough. It's not easy. It's never easy. But if you don't do this... Aoife, you have to be strong to survive—"

"There's being strong, and there's fucking murdering your friend in cold blood for no fucking reason."

"But there *is* a reason, Aoife. Don't you see? If we're ever going to get out of this mess—if humanity is ever going to get out of this mess—then how are we ever going to survive and thrive if we haven't learned something? If we haven't got stronger as a result?"

She looked into Christopher's wide brown eyes, and right then, for the first time, she actually thought he looked and sounded insane. The thing that had unsettled her most about him before now was just how calm and measured he sounded. How genuinely remorseful and regretful he sounded.

But right now, with all he was saying about humanity learning and getting stronger from this... she was beginning to see the cracks of grandeur in his personality, bubbling underneath.

"Who are you to decide who lives and who dies? Who are you to decide what becomes of humanity at all?"

Christopher sighed. "Aoife. Please. You've come so far in such a short space of time. Don't let emotion get to you now. Or attachment. This... this man here. Max. I wanted him to be strong enough too. Really. I mean that. But he isn't. So there's no choice. It's already decided anyway. His fate is already sealed. The question is, are you with us? Or are you not?"

She looked at Max. Saw him kneeling there. Saw how he wasn't saying a thing. Only staring at her.

And that made it all the more tough. Because he wasn't begging for his life. He wasn't saying a word. He wasn't fighting.

Was he trying in his best way to *encourage* her?

"You know what you need to do," Max said.

They were the first words he'd spoken.

The first words he'd spoken this entire ordeal.

And just hearing them made Aoife's heart sink.

Because they confirmed her suspicions.

They confirmed her fears.

Christopher looked around at Max. Then back at Aoife. His eyes narrowing, just a little. Like he didn't really understand that exchange.

And it was then that Aoife realised why Max was being so silent.

He didn't want to raise any suspicion.

He was doing this for her.

"Do it, Aoife. Or don't," Christopher said. "But remember, whatever you decide here... Max's fate is already sealed. Wouldn't you rather be the one to do it?"

She looked at the knife in Christopher's hand.

Looked up, over at Max.

Her teeth chattering together.

Her throat tightening, her eyes beginning to water.

Because she couldn't do this.

She couldn't lose Max.

She couldn't—

"Think about everyone else," Max whispered. "Remember what this is about."

She looked at him and shook her head. Her eyes filled with tears. Her heart racing so fast she thought she might just have a panic attack.

She looked at him, and it was as if it was only him and her here, now.

Only the pair of them.

He looked up at her, tears cascading down his face. And he smiled back at her. "You're strong, Aoife. So strong. Do what you need to do. For you. And for everyone. Remember? For everyone."

She shook her head. Tried to speak. But she couldn't say a word.

She could only focus on Max.

Only stare into those eyes that made her feel so safe.

So comfortable.

"For everyone," Max said. Crying now. "For—"

"I love you," Aoife said.

She wasn't sure where it came from. But it came. And when she said it, it surprised even herself.

She could see the surprise on Max's face, too. The way his smile dropped. And then the way it rose again. His eyes bloodshot. Covered in tears. "I love you too," he said.

She closed her burning eyes.

Gritted her teeth.

Then Aoife did the only thing she could do in this situation.

She grabbed the knife, and she walked over to Max.

# CHAPTER THIRTY-SEVEN

Aoife grabbed the knife and walked over to Max.

The walk was fucking torturous. She could feel the heat growing more and more suffocating. She could see people looking all around her. Watching her. Chatting amongst themselves.

And she could feel Max's eyes on her. Staring at her through every second.

Time moved so slow. And yet not slow enough.

She couldn't believe she was doing this.

Couldn't believe she was even entertaining doing this as tears poured down her face.

She felt like shit. Like total fucking shit.

But she felt trapped.

Like this was the only thing she could do.

Like there was no other way.

Like there was no other hope.

If she didn't do this, then everyone here would die. Herself included.

All the people who had been captured from the estate would die.

And any hope of escaping this place, slim as it was, would be over.

She stepped right up to Max. Stood right before him. Clutched the knife loosely in her shaking hand.

He looked right up at her. Tears falling down his cheeks.

But a smile on his face.

A smile on that rough, worn face of his.

He looked proud of her.

"I wish there were another way," he said. "Really wish there was. But there isn't. And this is all we've got. So you fight, Aoife. You make sure you fight. You know what I'm talking about. Exactly what I'm talking about."

She looked down at him, and she couldn't contain herself. Couldn't control the emotion spilling out of her. She looked around at Christopher, who stared on. Half expected him to say this was just a test, like the whole making her eat meat thing before.

But this looked for real.

This wasn't a rehearsal.

This was the real thing.

And she needed to do what she needed to do.

"It was Jason," she whispered, turning back to Max.

Max frowned. "What?"

"The man I killed in there. It was Jason. My ex."

Max's eyes narrowed, then widened. The realisation. The realisation in his eyes about what Aoife was talking about; what she was referring to.

"Damn," Max said. "I'm glad. Was starting to think you were a full-blown psychopath for a moment. At least it was a nonce who deserved it."

And Aoife laughed. Despite the horror of the situation, despite what she knew she was being asked to do, she actually laughed through her tears.

"Come on," the woman behind said. The one with the red hair

who'd threatened and choked Aoife not long ago. "This really necessary?"

"Cassandra," Christopher said. "They're friends. They're close. They... they deserve a goodbye. This isn't easy on Aoife. Have a bit of compassion."

Aoife heard them speaking and came crashing right back down to earth. Because this wasn't a rehearsal. This wasn't a test run. This was it.

"Remember what I told you," Max said.

"I remember a lot of shit you told me, you idiot," she said, through snotty cries. "Be more specific."

Max grunted. "About... about connections. About how... about how avoiding making connections is—"

"Avoiding living. Yeah."

"Do you regret that we met? That we got close? Do you regret any of that?"

Aoife looked down into Max's eyes. And as much as she knew what was coming, as much as the reality was dawning on her—the reality that she was going to lose him... and as much as it was going to break her, as painful and as unimaginable as it was going to be... she shook her head.

"I don't regret a thing."

Max nodded. And he genuinely smiled, too. "Then remember that. Remember it in your darkest moments. Remember it when it feels like—when it feels like there's no hope. Just remember this moment. And remember that feeling."

She stood there. Right opposite him. Knife in her shaking hand.

"Now do it. And make it quick. And then... and then you don't get sloppy, Aoife. You understand? You don't get sloppy. Not when it comes to the lives of our people."

And Aoife nodded. She could barely even focus. Barely even process any of what was happening anymore. It didn't feel real. None of this felt real.

But it *was* real.

And it was the only way out.

She walked around the back of Max. She stood there. Looked down at him, only at him. The anxiety taking hold. Breathing getting harder.

Knife shaking in her hand violently.

Christopher standing opposite, looming in the distance.

Everyone else looming in the distance as the sun beat down from above.

"I love you, Aoife," Max said. His voice shaking. But sounding... happy. Sounding content. "And meeting you was the best-damned thing that's happened to me since Kathryn. Since David. And if I... if it were a choice between dying now after spending the last six months with you or living the life I lived before the power went out, I wouldn't change a thing. Thank you. Thank you."

She closed her eyes. Squeezed them shut. She wanted to speak. She wanted to tell him how much she loved him. She wanted to apologise. She wanted to thank him.

But in the end, she couldn't.

She could only cry.

And the only words she could say: "I love you. Thank you. Thank you. I'm sorry. I'm sorry."

She lifted the knife to his throat.

She felt the warmth of his skin.

The warmth of the sun beating down.

"I love you. I'm sorry. I'm..."

"I love you too. I love you too."

She felt Max's presence, close.

A father figure.

A lover.

She felt him close, and right there, in her heart.

"Do what you have to do," he said. "What you know you have to..."

And then her eyes opened.

She lowered the knife.

Stepped back.

Max looked around.

Everyone looked around.

"What?" Christopher said.

"I can't do it," Aoife said.

Max glared at her. "But Aoife—"

"I can't do it. I'm sorry. I can't do it. I... I can't do this. I just can't."

She saw Cassandra's head lower.

She saw Christopher sigh.

"That's unfortunate," he said. "You really had potential. Cassandra?"

Cassandra looked up.

Nodded.

Walked over towards Max.

Knife in her hand.

But Aoife wasn't letting this happen.

She wasn't letting any of this happen.

She saw the two people approaching her, coming to restrain her, and she knew she had one shot.

She launched herself at Cassandra.

Punched her across the face.

Then she wrapped her arm around Cassandra's throat and held the knife to her neck.

"We're leaving this place," Aoife spat. "Me and Max are leaving this fucking place. Or I cut her throat, right here."

## CHAPTER THIRTY-EIGHT

"Put the knife down, Aoife. Put it down. There's no need for hysterics right now. Just be calm and think about what you're doing here. Very carefully."

Aoife held on to Cassandra and pushed the blade right into her throat. Cassandra kept on wriggling, trying to break free, but the bitch wasn't going anywhere.

Aoife was leaving this place.

Max was leaving this place.

"Aoife." That was Max. He was speaking to her. Kneeling there with wide eyes.

Two people walked over towards him, clearly trying to restrain him.

"Not another fucking move," Aoife said. Pushing the blade in deeper.

Christopher stepped forward. "Aoife, this isn't the road you want to go down—"

"It is the road I want to go down," Aoife shouted. "So don't stand there and tell me what I want to do or don't want to do. You aren't killing Max. And you aren't—you aren't killing me. This isn't how this ends."

Christopher shook his head. Sighed. "Aoife... don't do this. I thought you saw our way. I thought you saw this isn't how any of us *want* things to be. It's just the way it *has* to be."

"What gave you the right to decide? What gives you the right to decide what's best for humanity? What's best for all of us?"

"Nobody gave me any right," Christopher said. "But sometimes in life, you have to stand up, and you have to do the impossible thing. Because if you don't, if you aren't willing to do the impossible thing, then society just collapses."

"You're really full of it," Aoife shouted. "Aren't you? The lot of you. You're—you're full of it."

"We see the way things have to be," Christopher said. "The only way things *can* be. Put the knife down. It's over. And the longer you do this, the more you're only condemning yourself."

Aoife looked at Christopher. At Max. Then at the people gathered around. She looked over her shoulder, over at the fences. At the gap between the fence. She could make it there. Get there and escape that way.

And then they could come back here, and they could help the rest of the people here. The people from the estate.

They could save them.

"If this is a road you want to go down," Christopher said. "Then that's your choice. But this only ends one way for you, Aoife. This only ends one way for you, and it only ends one way for Max. If this is the road you've chosen."

She held the knife to Cassandra's struggling neck.

Looked at Max, who stared back at her.

"Put the blade down," Christopher said. "And this can still have a different outcome."

She looked at him. And she could see from the look in his eyes that he was weak. He was afraid.

She looked back at Max.

"Be ready," she whispered.

And then she sliced Cassandra's throat.

"Now," she shouted.

She turned around. Ran. Looked back and saw Max running behind her, too. And behind them, as Cassandra dropped to the floor spluttering on her own blood, the group approaching. Closing in. But in panic.

But Christopher was running.

Christopher was chasing them.

And he wasn't far behind Max.

"Come on," Aoife shouted, turning back to the fence. Heart racing. Adrenaline surging. Only just realising that she was half-naked. She legged it towards that gap in the fence. Felt like she was running in tar. Wished she could run faster. There had to be a way out. There just had to be.

She slipped. Tripped up. Grazed her knees.

And she started to lose hope when she felt a hand on her back.

Turned around.

Half-expected Christopher.

But it was Max.

"Get up," he said. "Get up and run for your life. I love you, Aoife. I love you."

She felt him pick her up.

And she started to run when she realised something.

When something hit her.

Christopher.

He was right behind Max now.

So close to him.

Closing in on him.

Too close for Max to get away.

"I can't leave you—"

"You aren't leaving me," Max said. Tearful. But a proud smile on his face. "You're saving everyone here. Now go, Aoife. Go!"

She looked at Max, and she wanted to stay here with him.

She wanted to fight for him.

But then she knew he was right.

She had no choice.

"I'm sorry," she said.

"Don't be sorry. You're going to save so many because of this."

She opened her mouth to say something else to him when it all happened so fast.

Christopher appeared behind him.

Right behind him.

Some of Christopher's people ran past him and Max, chasing Aoife.

She looked right into Max's eyes.

Then she shook her head, turned, and ran away.

She sprinted to the fence.

Sprinted even though she heard footsteps closing in, getting closer.

Sprinted and sprinted even though she could barely see through the tears.

And then she dragged herself through the fence, felt the sharp edges of it scratching against her skin, tearing at her.

When she looked back around, she saw the blade against Max's throat.

She looked away.

She couldn't look anymore.

She could only run.

She knew it was over.

Max was gone.

## CHAPTER THIRTY-NINE

Aoife walked through the woods.

It was bright. Morning. Far too bright. Gave her a headache. Her legs were aching. Her chest was tight. And she was exhausted. Totally exhausted.

She just wanted to roll over and sleep. To pass out into unconsciousness.

She just wanted to drink and to forget.

The image that wouldn't leave her mind.

The image of running away from Christopher. Running away from his people.

Turning around. Seeing Max standing there. Seeing Christopher right behind him.

Seeing that knife to his neck...

And knowing what would've come next.

She knew there was no more reason for them to keep him around. To keep him alive. After all, they'd told her that his death was inevitable. That's why they'd tried to make her kill him in the first place.

But now, as she wandered through the woods, she felt lost, and she felt alone.

Because without Max, what was the point in anything anymore?

He was the one person she cared about. He was the one who kept her grounded. Kept her strong. And made her feel safe, even when they didn't agree on things.

He was the one who'd taught her that she could bond with people again. That she didn't have to be so stubborn. That there was more to life than she'd resigned herself to think.

He'd changed her life in so many ways he didn't even realise.

And now he was gone.

She stopped. Saw the outline of his home in the distance. She wasn't sure what'd drawn her here. Just that she felt a sense of duty to come here. Some kind of strange sense of responsibility.

Because there was nothing she could do to help the people trapped by Christopher.

There was nothing she could gain by going back to the estate. There was nothing there for her but shame. The shameful reminders of what she'd lost. Of the decisions she'd made and how much they'd cost her—cost everyone.

She should have put her foot down. She should have stopped the estate group leaving for the bullshit safe haven.

She should have done so, so much more.

And then at the abattoir. She could have fought harder. She could have helped Max. She could have saved him.

But now she was here. On her own. Running away, once again. The sole survivor, once again.

What did that make her?

Did it make her any better than a cockroach, really?

She was always the last one left. And maybe that meant she was a true survivor. Maybe she was the best kind of person to live in this world. Because she was useless. Useless at looking after people. Useless at saving people.

And for that reason, she was better off just going her own way.

Better off just surviving on her own.

Drinking as much as possible.

Disappearing into the oblivious void that gave her the most peace in this world.

She stumbled further through the woods, feet aching, blisters impossibly painful, when she saw it up ahead.

It'd been a long time since she'd been here. But it was exactly the same as she remembered. Sure, the grass outside was long. And it looked like the windows needed a good clean.

But it was recognisable in an instant.

Max's place.

She felt a knot in her stomach. A lump in her throat. She felt tears building up. She'd come here because she wanted to be as close to him as she could be. That's what it was. That's the only thing she could make sense of.

She'd come here because she felt like she was lost without him.

She looked at the house, shaking. Shivering. She looked back over her shoulder. Back towards the direction she'd come from. Towards the abattoir. And she asked herself the question, was there more she could do? Was there more she could have done?

And then she looked around, down the slope, down to where she knew the estate was.

Was there more she could do there?

Was there more she could do to help?

And then her stomach dropped.

What more could she do?

And did she even *want* to do anything anymore?

She couldn't do anything.

And she was the fucking kiss of death anyway.

Why would she possibly want to be close to anyone again when she just lost everyone?

And why would anyone want to be close to her when shit seemed to happen to everyone closest to her?

She looked around at the woods. Listened to the wind blowing against the trees. Thought about the day she'd got here. The day she'd reached his house.

And as much shit had gone down in the hours before, and the hours that followed... she would never forget feeling that sense of total peace.

That sense of happiness.

That sense that her life had been missing something, and now she'd found it, all over again.

She thought about what Max said about not wanting to trade anything for the connection they'd had, and as much as she agreed with the sentiment... the pain was just so strong that she wasn't sure she agreed.

She wasn't sure the pain was worth it.

The last conversation they'd had before all this in the woods.

What she'd said about his family...

She shook her head and felt the allure of alcohol.

She was alone.

No Max.

No Rex.

Nobody.

She looked around. Back at the house.

Took a long, deep breath.

And through tearful, resigned pain, she walked towards it.

There was no outside world for her anymore.

There was nobody at all for her anymore.

This was her life now.

## CHAPTER FORTY

Christopher looked out at the woods and tensed his fists.

He could see the trees up ahead. They made him feel calm. He loved the woods. Always reminded him of being a child. Running freely with his brothers either side of him. Stick fights. Sometimes, Mum would join in, and they'd all have an amazing time.

He'd had a good childhood, all things considered. Of course, they were poor, especially after Dad walked out on them early. Mum struggled, but he was oblivious to that as a child, so he couldn't say it affected him in any way. There wasn't anything tragic in his past. Nothing major, anyway. There was nothing he could complain about. He'd had a relatively normal upbringing, a relatively normal life.

He looked down at the blade in his hand, shaking away. And then he thought back to the chase just then. Saw some of his people stepping beyond the gates in pursuit of Aoife.

And as he stood there and watched, he felt a horrible pain in the middle of his chest.

A realisation of the horror of what he was doing.

A realisation of how wrong it was.

Because he wasn't a killer. He wasn't anything near a killer.

He was just trying to survive. He was just trying his best to survive, and to help as many people as possible survive, too.

He hated what he did. Hated himself for it. Felt the pains on his back. The scars. The scars he gave himself, every night, along with a shot of whisky.

His self-punishment for everything he put people through.

His punishment for everything he did.

The tears.

The screams.

And the nightmares.

Oh, the nightmares.

And he wasn't trying to make himself a fucking martyr or anything. He knew what he did was reprehensible. Morally unforgivable.

But if he had to be the one to make the choices he made, and if humanity had a shot at surviving because of it... then he'd make that sacrifice.

"Chris?"

Christopher looked around. Saw Trent approaching. His eyes were wide. His face looked paler than usual, which was hard to imagine considering he was always pale as a ghost.

He looked at Christopher with sadness to his face.

"Yes?" Christopher said.

"What do you want us to do with her?"

When he said those words, Christopher's heart sank. Cassandra. She was a loyal woman. And he'd felt something for her. Felt close to her. Sure, they were different. And there was something about her that scared him a bit; he couldn't deny it.

But she was one of his people.

She was one of his closest friends.

And she was ruthless. What he lacked in ruthlessness, she certainly more than made up for.

And yet, he felt conflicted. Because it wasn't her death he felt empty about.

It was Aoife's escape he felt emptier about.

That wasn't something he could share with the rest of the people here. It would be too complicated. Too problematic.

But there was something about Aoife.

Some feeling he had for her that he couldn't put his finger on.

He thought she was strong.

He thought she was on board.

He thought she could see why they were doing what they were doing.

And then she'd thrown it right back in his face, right at the death.

He thought about how Max had been the only obstacle in his mind. Get him out of the way, and then maybe they could move forward. Together one day, perhaps.

He knew how ridiculous he sounded. He knew how childish and immature he sounded.

But screw it. He'd never had a proper girlfriend in his entire adult life, and he wanted one.

And hell, maybe it was time to start being a little more forceful on that front. Mum always told him he lacked assertiveness, and that held him back.

Maybe it was time to start being more assertive.

Maybe it was time to change even more in line with the changed rules.

The changed world.

He was thirty-one, after all.

"There's no point wasting her," Christopher said.

Trent's face dropped just for a second. "But—but she's one of our own. We don't—"

"It's what Cassandra would have wanted. Make use of her. It's in her honour."

He turned away from Trent. He didn't want to talk about the matter. Not anymore.

Then he looked around at the woods again.

At the people heading back out there, towards Aoife.

He felt that urge. That need to find her again. That need to bring her back.

And as painful as it was and as selfish as it was, he had a feeling he knew *exactly* what would bring her back.

He turned. Walked across the yard, over to the Factory. Walked down the dark, dingy corridors, past those who were in their pens, those who would feed their people—in time.

And then he walked over to the metal door, right at the back of the corridor, and opened it.

He looked inside there.

Saw him sitting there.

"Hello, Max."

Max sat there in the corner of the room.

Naked. Covered in sweat. Shaking.

He looked at Max, and he told himself not to be sympathetic. He told himself to be assertive. To stand up for himself.

And he felt that jealousy, too.

Because this went beyond mere pragmatism.

This was personal now.

He walked over to Max.

Crouched right before him.

Knife in his hand.

Looked into his eyes as he sat there, chained to a pipe at the back of the wall.

"We'll figure something out," Christopher said. "But it isn't over yet. It isn't over by any stretch of the imagination."

He saw Max's eyes squinting.

Saw him gritting his teeth.

Saw him trying to say something from underneath his gag.

Christopher took a deep breath.

And as disgusted as he was by himself... he fell into that void now.

Into that darkness he'd pushed back against for so, so long.

"I can't wait to taste you," Christopher said. "You'll look particularly dashing on a meat hook."

He saw Max's eyes widen.

Saw him struggling.

Heard him trying to speak and shout again.

And Christopher just stood up.

Slammed the door behind Max.

Walked away.

He stood there, heart racing. Tensed his fists.

And when he looked into the reflective wall to his right, cracked down the middle, he swore he saw himself smiling.

# CHAPTER FORTY-ONE

Aoife gulped back the neat vodka and felt its warmth engulfing her already.

She had no idea what time it was. Had a vague sense that she was at Max's place, but the details were fuzzy, blurry. She didn't care about anything, and that's how she liked it, really. The booze was strong. So strong she could feel it burning her nostrils as she breathed. She kept on hiccupping, tasting a little bit of sick, and laughing.

This was where she felt good.

This was where she felt best.

This was where she felt at home.

She gulped back more of Max's vodka and looked across the room, over at the fireplace. She couldn't be bothered lighting it. If she lit it, she'd probably end up setting the whole fucking house on fire.

And would that be such a bad thing, really?

At least if she set the house on fire, and she was swallowed and burned up by it all, wouldn't that just be the best way to end her misery, really?

She laughed again. What was the saying about something

screaming in a wood and nobody hearing it? A bear shitting in the woods? She didn't know. Wasn't sure. Too fucking drunk to care.

She just sat here, the burning taste of booze in her mouth, and she smiled.

At least she was comfortable here.

At least she was happy here.

She gulped back more of the drink and realised the bottle was empty. Shit. She must've gone right through it all in no time at all.

Oh well. Not to worry. Max had more booze.

And if there was one way to honour him, Aoife was certain that booze was the way.

She got up. Stumbled forward, almost losing her footing. Laughed again. Everything felt very amusing right now. Very funny.

She held out her hands and waded her way across the front room. It felt like she was swimming. When she blinked, she suddenly jumped forward a few steps. Or that's what it felt like anyway.

Life didn't feel real. And she liked it that way.

Because at least this way, she didn't have to worry about what had happened.

She didn't have to worry about any kind of responsibilities.

She didn't have to worry about—

A bang.

Footsteps.

Somewhere in the house.

She froze. The hairs on her arms stood on end, tingling with electricity.

She wasn't sure if she'd imagined it or not. But she was sure she'd heard something.

And it was in the house.

With her.

She looked over at the doorway leading to the back of the house. It came from there, she could swear.

She stepped forward. Shaking. Finding it hard to focus, hard to coordinate. God, it was difficult walking. One foot in front of the other, and it felt like the hardest task in the world.

She laughed again. Burped up some more booze, some more sick. As much as she was scared... she could still feel some humour. Still found herself giggling. Mumbling under her breath.

Probably all in her head. Probably all in her imagination.

She walked into the corridor, which seemed to be expanding around her, when she saw movement in the kitchen.

It was quick. And it was... low. As if someone was crawling through the house.

And truth be told, it creeped her out. It made her feel vulnerable. It made her feel afraid.

She didn't feel like laughing anymore.

"Hello?" she said.

She walked further down the corridor. Tried to put her hands on the walls either side of her to support herself, but it didn't help much.

The hairs on her neck standing on end.

The danger—or potential danger—seeming to fly towards her quicker than she could think.

Quicker than she could think to stop herself.

She stumbled to the doorway.

Reached it and stood there, barely able to keep her footing.

She had to look.

She had to see.

She wasn't stupid. She knew Christopher's people would be out there. Probably looking for her.

At least if they came for her, she was too drunk to give a fuck what happened to her.

She was ready.

Prepared.

She stepped across the threshold, into the kitchen, and stopped.

It was dark in here. Dusty. Grey. Pots and pans everywhere. Old plates stacked up, which flies buzzed around.

She looked around the kitchen and saw the door to the little laundry room twitch, just a little.

She walked over to the side of the kitchen. Grabbed a knife, quietly.

If they were in there, she'd be ready for them.

She'd be ready for them, and she'd take them down.

Or she'd go the hell down fighting.

She walked as quietly and as subtly as she could across the kitchen.

Towards that door.

Held her breath.

Shaking.

But ready.

Adrenaline surging.

*Alive.*

She put a shaky hand on the handle.

Gritted her teeth.

Held her breath.

And then she pulled the door open and lifted her knife.

When she saw who—what—was there, the knife dropped from her clutches in an instant.

He was backed up against the wall.

Looking up at her with those big brown eyes.

Wagging his tail.

"Rex?" she said.

He stepped out, then. But his ears were low. He looked a shadow of the dog she'd grown to know. More like his old, nervous self.

And as much as she felt the pain, as much as she felt the resistance to connect, to bond, as much as she just wanted to be on her own... she felt relieved.

She felt happy.

She felt so, so happy to see him.

She stood there, lips quivering, eyes stinging.

And then she couldn't help herself and couldn't stop herself.

"Come here, lad. Come here."

Rex rushed over to her.

Landed in her arms.

And she held him, cuddled his warm body close, ruffled his fur, and she cried.

# CHAPTER FORTY-TWO

Aoife opened her eyes.

It was light. Really fucking bright light, for that matter. Her head was banging. Her throat was sore. She felt sick. So damned sick. Could taste vomit in her mouth. And the side of her head hurt—bad. Felt like she'd slept on a bloody hard floor or something.

She blinked a few times, tried to get her bearings. Then she opened her eyes, not as incapacitated by the brightness anymore, and looked around.

She realised she felt like she'd slept on a bloody hard floor because she *was* on a bloody hard floor. The hard floor of... Max's house?

She looked around. Oh no. Max. She knew what'd happened to him.

She closed her eyes. Squeezed them shut. Heart racing.

She'd got drunk last night. Very drunk. She could smell vomit in the air and taste it, dry on her lips, and it made her want to throw up even more. She'd come back to Max's, found all the bottles of hard liquor she could find, and she'd downed the lot of it.

Looked like she'd passed out at some point, just before she could give herself alcohol poisoning.

She wasn't sure what the best outcome would have been. The way she felt right now, she thought being poisoned might not be such a bad alternative after all.

She held her breath. Her head split with pain. Her chest was tight, and she felt weak and dizzy.

And the worst thing at all?

Through all this pain, she just wanted to drink more.

To put herself back into that blissful state of unconsciousness.

Because anything was better than how she felt now.

Now she was awake, now she was conscious... she knew the reminders would arrive again soon.

The reminders of what she'd lost.

She went to head to the kitchen when she heard movement in the corner of the room.

Nails scratching against the floor.

She looked and saw Rex standing there.

It hit her, then. Rex. Part of her thought it was a dream. But she remembered finding him, remembered holding him, remembered crying into his fur and stroking him.

But seeing him here, wagging his tail, tongue dangling out... she could have no illusions over the fact he was real.

He was real, he was here, and he was alive.

"Hey," she said. "Good lad. Good..."

Burning sensation right up her throat.

She turned, went to run towards the bathroom.

But she couldn't help herself.

She vomited everywhere. All over the floor.

And as she crouched there, shaking on her hands and knees, she felt like total shit. Like a total failure. Was this what had become of her life? Was this what her dad would have wanted of her?

Is this what Max would want of her?

She wiped the vomit from her mouth and squeezed her burning eyes shut again.

She didn't care what anyone wanted of her.

This was exactly who she was.

This was exactly what she deserved.

This was...

She felt it, then.

The nudge.

She opened her eyes.

Saw Rex nudging his head against her arm.

Like he was trying to comfort her.

Like he knew she was upset, and he wanted to make her feel better.

She looked at him, and in that instant, as he looked at her with his big brown eyes, something struck her.

Out of nowhere, she heard them. Words. Words in her ears. Words she'd heard recently.

Words she'd heard from Max.

*"Avoiding connecting is avoiding living. You have to embrace it, highs and lows..."*

She heard those words, and she saw Rex beside her, and she flashed back to the first time she'd seen Rex.

Saving him from those thugs.

Rescuing him.

Giving him another chance at life.

And here he was.

She hadn't lost everybody. Because here he was.

Still here.

All because she'd given him another chance.

She felt Rex nudging against her shaking arm, and she cuddled him. She stroked him. She let him be there for her. Felt his warmth.

And the longer she held him, the more she felt like everything was becoming clearer.

Like it was all making more sense.

She'd pushed people away out of fear.

She'd pushed them away, and yet here Rex still was.

And Max's words. Max was right.

Avoiding connecting was avoiding living.

He had to be right because he'd been here—right here, where she was—himself.

And he'd got himself out of it.

She held on to Rex, and she felt herself smiling amidst the tears. Because it wasn't over. It couldn't be over.

There were still people at the abattoir. People from the estate.

And there would be people at the estate too. People who'd escaped Christopher's assault.

And even though Max was gone... he was right.

She was still here.

Which meant she still had a chance.

The very fact she'd got away, she'd escaped, meant there was a chance that she could defeat Christopher.

That she could rescue people.

That she could end Christopher's sick, twisted dominance.

She stood up. Looked down at Rex. And through the banging headache, through all of it, she felt strength surge through her body.

"We're going to nail that bastard," she said, looking at Rex. "We're going to finish that fucker. And we're going to enjoy every second of it."

## CHAPTER FORTY-THREE

Oliver stared at the meagre bowl of squirrel stew right in front of him and wasn't sure how long he was gonna survive on this alone.

It was morning, and it was hot. Really damned hot. Times like these, he wanted nothing more than to be inside, under some nice air conditioning. Never used to like the stifling heat. His wife, Betty, always used to whinge at him for it. While she'd be out on the balcony in their apartment in Spain, he'd be inside, reading a book.

She used to take the piss. But at the end of the day, she was the one who'd end up burned. Fried by the sun.

He smiled when he thought of Betty. That hole in his life that was there ever since she passed away two months ago. The sickness. Never wanted the old vaccine for COVID, and it probably was the death of her in the end.

Damned virus. Some invisible little bastard stealing the love of his life from him. If he could strangle the shit, he would do.

But now, as he looked down at the tiny puddle of water and the chewy-looking lump of squirrel meat in the bowl before him, he kind of thought Betty had got off this life train at exactly the right time. Better to go fairly quickly and with a shred of dignity than to have your humanity slowly stripped away like this.

Starving slowly.

Dehydrating.

He looked up at Cal, who stood there, serving spoon in hand. He looked gaunt like he'd gone grey overnight. He offered an attempt at a smile, but he wasn't fooling nobody.

"Sorry, Oliver," he said. "I really wish we had more."

Oliver nodded. Smiled back at him. "You're doing your best." He was cooperative, but not everybody would be.

That said, when Oliver looked back at the line for the food, it struck him just how much this place had been rocked by the last few days.

Half of the people from this place, missing, just like that.

Some kind of ambush in the woods.

He had no idea who'd been captured. No idea how many had just fled and not come back here. But he'd made it back here, and so too had about twenty others.

The very fact that the supplies they had remaining here weren't even enough to feed twenty was a real dire sign of just how deep the shit they were in really was.

"This is bullshit," a voice said.

Oliver looked round. Saw Geoff, a big guy who seemed to be permanently sweaty, kicking off at Cal.

"Geoff," Cal said. "I'm sorry. If there were more, I'd give you more."

Geoff slammed the plate of food to the ground, something which sparked fury amongst the rest of the crowd.

"We should be out there," Geoff said. "We should be finding somewhere new. Hell, we should be playing by new rules if that's what it comes to. But this is bullshit. We're all gonna die here. And we're just accepting it. We're just fucking accepting it."

Oliver didn't like Geoff. Didn't like his way of speaking, his way of going about things. And he thought he was a real dick for throwing that food on the ground right now, especially when food was in such short supply.

But at the same time... the hardest thing to swallow was that there was some truth to what Geoff was saying.

They were on a one-way road to Deadsville if they stayed here. Just accepted their fate.

And yet...

What happened out there in the woods had scared everybody in here.

Because who knew who those people were?

Who knew what they wanted?

And who knew when they were going to strike again?

"Geoff," Oliver said.

Geoff turned around to Oliver. Scanned him, head to toe, like he was eyeing up a competitor in a boxing match. "What the hell do you want?"

"Just cool it. We're all in this together."

Geoff walked over to Oliver slowly. But his fists were clenched, and he looked set to knock Oliver's head from his shoulders.

"Let's not tear each other apart. It's about the only good thing we've got left."

"Yeah?" Geoff said. "You really think so? Fat fucking load of good it's done us."

He turned around, then. Looked at the small crowd of people who had gathered.

"The way I see it, we've got a choice here. We stay here, and we keep on moping the fuck around. Or we get out there, and we start looking for someplace new. And if we have to take it from somebody else, well, we have to take it from somebody else. You know it's the right thing. About time we started breaking a few rules. 'Cause this world ain't about making friends. And the sooner you lot wake the fuck up and realise that, the better."

A few people shook their heads. "But it's our home!"

But enough people nodded.

Enough people cheered.

Enough people were on board.

And as much as Oliver appreciated the sentiment... he knew for a fact that going out there charged by adrenaline and hot-headedness wasn't gonna get them anywhere but killed.

Especially following the lead of a useless bastard like Geoff.

"So what exactly is your plan?" Oliver asked.

Geoff looked around again. Narrowed his eyes. "You what?"

"I asked a question. What exactly is your plan?"

"What does it matter to you?"

"It matters to me because I'm one of the people living here. And I happen to care about everybody here. Not just myself."

Everywhere went quiet. A few mutters, a few whispers.

And a feeling in the pit of Oliver's stomach that shit might just kick off any time.

Geoff's eyelids twitched. "What're you trying to say?"

Oliver's heart thudded. But he was too far in to back out now. "I'm just saying... whatever we decide, it needs to be a proper plan. A plan that works for everybody. Not just hot-headedness that gets us killed."

A couple of louder mutters, mostly sounding nervous.

Geoff's face flushed a bit. "Calling me a hot head?"

Oliver looked at Geoff. Then around at this small crowd.

Then, he took a breath and threw caution to the bloody wind. "Yeah. Yeah, in fact, I am."

Some tuts. Some claps.

But an overriding sense that the mood was getting more and more sour.

Oliver saw Geoff walk closer to him. So close that he could smell that sickly sweet sweat from his glistening face. Some of it congealing in his beard.

"Tell me then, smart guy," Geoff said. "What do you suggest?"

Oliver looked him right in the eyes. "It's not for *me* to decide.

It's for *us* to decide. But the way I see it... even though we don't have much food left. Even though things are bad. It's the best place we've got, still. And until we find someplace better... it's home. So we'll have to make it work."

Oliver hoped for more claps. For more unity. But it was so damned quiet you could probably hear that proverbial pin drop.

Geoff seemed to notice this too, 'cause his face lit up for a second. "Or maybe it's about time we stopped listening to indecisive pricks like you. 'Cause it's your type who got us into this mess in the first place."

And those words *did* get some applause.

Applause that made Oliver's stomach sink.

'Cause it felt like they were on a one-way path to destruction now.

Especially with the leadership void that had opened up in the wake of Kathy's disappearance.

Geoff turned around. Faced his semi-adoring crowd.

"It's about time the strong and silent stood up for themselves. About time we did something differently around here. 'Cause if we don't, we're finished. If we don't, we're dead."

More claps. More applause.

Geoff turned around. Looked right at Oliver, with total disdain.

"So you weak fuckers can stay right here and rot if you want to. But we're gonna go out there. We're gonna find ourselves a new home. And if you think we're gonna share what we have with you... you're mistaken. 'Cause it ain't yours anymore. It ain't—"

"We're not going anywhere," a voice said.

Oliver didn't recognise it. Not at first.

In fact, it seemed to startle everyone. Take everyone by surprise. 'Cause it came out of nowhere.

Geoff looked around.

The crowd turned around.

Everyone looked around.

And when Oliver saw who was standing there, he frowned.

Skinny. Long, dark hair. Dressed in man's clothes, clearly too big and baggy for her.

Dog by her side.

"What did you say?" Geoff asked.

The girl, Aoife, looked right at Geoff, then at Oliver, then at the rest of the people here.

"We're not going anywhere without a plan," Aoife said. "To get the rest of our people back. And to destroy the bastards who took them from us."

# CHAPTER FORTY-FOUR

Aoife stood at the entrance to the estate, Rex by her side, and prepared herself to give the most important speech of her life.

She looked at the crowd of people gathered in the sun. She'd seen things getting a little hairy and out of control. Mostly instigated by a guy called Geoff, by the looks of things, a bloke she didn't know well but was fully aware was a kind of stereotypically British middle-aged boozer with a pot belly and a tattoo of a Union Jack on his sleeve.

Basically, her least favourite genre of man.

But it wasn't just Geoff looking at her with bewilderment right now. With bemusement.

It was everyone here.

And after all, she could get it. Because who the hell was she, really?

She'd spent the last six months hiding away in the shadows after the confrontation that took Nathan and Moira's lives. She'd spent the bulk of the time drinking, not contributing. So who was she to come in now and start dictating to the people here about how they should be going about things?

"What did you just say?" Geoff asked.

Aoife took a few breaths. Calmed herself as best as she could. "You have no idea what I've been through," she said, voice shaking. "What any of the rest of this group has been through. But I'll tell you. I'll tell you right now, just so you have an idea of the kind of threat we're facing."

"Look, Siobhan. Or Saoirse. Or whatever the hell weird spelled Irish name it is you're called. We appreciate your dramatics right now. But we're leaving this place. The decision's already been made—"

"It's Aoife. Not far from here, there's a group of people. Highly organised people. Led by a man called Christopher. You met him. We all did. He went by the name of Vincent. Remember him?"

A few frowns. A few whispers.

"They're pretty normal like us lot. If you met them in the world before, they'd probably seem decent people. The kind you'd want to hang out with. Have a pint with. Only there's a catch. They're hunting people. They're hunting them, and they're using them for meat. And in time... in time, they'll turn to farming us. Because after all, what easier livestock is there than hopeful people? People who've been given a glimmer of hope about some bullshit safe haven or other?"

The crowd before her was silent now. A few whispers amongst them like they were trying to get their heads around what Aoife was saying.

"They have our people," Aoife said. "Those of us who didn't make it back here, they're in captivity right now. And soon, I'm not sure when exactly, but soon... they will be killed. Some already have been killed. Amir, that I know of. And..." She gulped. "And Max."

She looked at the road. Tried not to lose her shit. Tried to keep her composure.

Took a deep breath and looked back at the crowd.

"If we don't stand together now, if we aren't strong now, then our people and our friends will die. And then we will die. Because make no mistake about it. Christopher's people might be as empathetic as a group of cannibals can be. But they are ruthless, and they are loyal. And they will come after us. They will. And the best way they can catch us is off guard. Is when we're all split up and separated. So the last thing we want to be doing right now is splitting up. The last thing we want to be doing is separating. Times may be hard, impossible even... but right now, we need to stick together. It might be the only way we survive. And it might be the only way we stop him. And save the rest of our people."

Silence followed again. Aoife didn't know what else to say. She didn't know where to go from here.

She just hoped she'd said enough.

It was Geoff who spoke first. "And why the hell should we believe you?"

He stepped forward. Everyone watched him. And it felt like people were waiting on the fence. Waiting to see how this whole debate unfolded.

"You come here six months ago. You bring nothing but trouble with you. And then you slink off into the shadows and drink yourself half to death every single day without contributing a goddamned thing. Why should we follow you?"

Aoife stood her ground. And as much as she hated this creep, she nodded. "You're right. I didn't exactly put the best account of myself across."

Geoff laughed. "Yeah. You've got that part right."

"But," Aoife said. "A friend taught me something." She closed her burning, stinging eyes. "He taught me that... that avoiding connecting is avoiding living. And we have such a good group here. But half of that group is in danger right now. Real danger. And if we leave them behind, if we abandon them... we're betraying everything good about ourselves that has got us this far."

A pause. A silence. One that Aoife didn't know how to interpret.

"I won't pretend I can't have been a better person. But I was the way I was because I was lost. And I was afraid. Afraid of connecting because I was afraid of losing. But... but I've seen the other way, now. I've seen that connection's the best thing we've got. And... and even if we lose it all, we have to try. We can't just not try. Because that's not who we are. You... you people never turned your backs on me, even with how shit I've been. We can't do the same for the rest of our people."

She looked at the crowd behind Geoff. Saw them looking at her. And she still found it hard gauging the mood. Figuring out how convinced they were.

That's when she saw a few of them nodding.

Heard them muttering in agreement.

A spark of hope inside her.

"We need to figure out how to defeat Christopher," she said. "And his people. And if we work together, all of us, I'm convinced we'll find a way. But we need to work together, and we need to work together fast. Or more people will die."

"And what if them dying ain't such a bad thing?" Geoff said.

Silence followed those words.

Aoife frowned. "What?"

Geoff shrugged. His cheeks were flushed, and he couldn't look Aoife in the eye anymore. "I'm just sayin'. We were overcrowded as it were. And it weren't our fault that lot got themselves captured. Maybe it's time we cut our losses. Fewer mouths to feed, more chance of living, and all that. Right?"

He looked around. Like he actually expected support.

But all he got were head shakes.

All he got were venomous glances.

All he got was disdain.

He looked back over at Aoife. Clearly frothing at the mouth but holding back. For now.

"We'll speak about this another time," Aoife said. "But for now... are you with me?"

He looked her in the eye.

Looked around.

Clearly so desperately wanted to shake his head. To say no.

And then his head just slumped.

He shook it. Rubbed his hand over his sweaty bald head.

"I just want to live. I just want... I just want all of us to live. I'm sorry."

She felt that apology. Felt the emotion in his voice. And as much as she didn't like the guy, she felt the sincerity. He just wanted what was best for those who were living. For himself. She'd been there herself. She couldn't hate him for that.

She looked over at the crowd. All of them looking at her now. Looking at her for direction.

Looking at her like she was a leader.

"So what now?" somebody said.

Aoife pushed aside the fear and stood tall. "We get ready," she said. "For war."

# CHAPTER FORTY-FIVE

Christopher stood at the top of the hill in the middle of the woods and looked down at the community in the distance.

It looked rather beautiful in the sun. The light seemed to shine right down the middle of the main road. Reminded him of childhood. Playing football on the quiet terraced roads with his brothers. The chime of the ice cream van. The rush to get that pound coin for a sugary delight before the van drove off. The taste of the sour sherbet, so refreshing, so delightful.

And then, moments later, he felt the punch in the gut.

The taste of meat.

The taste of flesh.

The smell of burning meat invading his senses, taking over...

He closed his eyes. His fists were clenched. He was sweating. Badly. He didn't feel good at all. Didn't feel good about the group he was leading. Didn't feel good about the processes they were going through.

But he didn't have to feel good about it.

He was the necessary martyr.

He was the one who knew the way.

He might not be popular for it. But in time, he'd be appreciated for it.

He was doing this for humanity. Really, he was.

It wasn't about himself.

He looked down at the small group of people gathered in the middle of that main street. About twenty of them, total.

The most interesting person?

Aoife.

She was there. She was there with her dog. The one who'd run off when his people ambushed.

She'd made it back here. Silly woman. Should have run far away from here.

For a moment, it looked a bit stand-offish between these people. Like they were at odds over something.

But then, eventually, they all came together.

All gathered together in a group.

And honestly, it made Christopher sad.

Because he knew what he needed to do.

He knew exactly what he needed to do.

It wasn't what he wanted to do.

But it was the only thing he could do.

He looked around.

Looked at Trent. At Darcey. Looked at all his people, standing there in the woods.

And then he looked at the people kneeling before them.

The men. The women. The old and the young.

Again, he felt a punch to the gut. This wasn't how he wanted to do things. He didn't want to use those captured from the estate as leverage. That wasn't how he or his people operated.

But he had to think outside the box. And he knew he could get them to stand down. He knew he could get them to surrender.

He looked in front of himself, and he saw probably the strongest one of the lot.

Max.

On his knees.

Christopher swallowed a lump in his throat. For a moment, he had something of an out of body experience.

Was he the villain here?

Was he the monster?

Hell, they were all monsters now.

They were no heroes now.

They were all just surviving.

He looked back over at the estate.

Then, he tightened his grip on his knife.

"Come on," he said. "It's time we paid our friends a visit. It's time we ended this."

## CHAPTER FORTY-SIX

Aoife stood right by the gates of the estate in front of her people.

It was mid-afternoon. The day felt like it was fast escaping them. It was hot, stiflingly so. And there was a weird tension in the air. A weird silence about the place. Like everyone was nervous. Apprehensive.

Probably because they were. After all, what they were about to do was scary. Terrifying, even.

They were about to take a leap of faith into the unknown, unlike they'd ever taken before.

They were about to go to battle.

"The plan is simple," Aoife said, "but that doesn't mean it's easy."

She looked at her people standing watch. Holding her to her every word. Even Geoff, who'd kicked up such a fuss earlier, seemed like he was on board now.

All of them were together. All of them were looking at her like she was filling some kind of leadership void.

And she was uncomfortable about that. Of course she bloody well was.

But you know what?

Sometimes in life, you have to do the uncomfortable things.

"We leave this place. All of us. We set up camps just outside the woods. We surround Christopher's people without them even realising we're surrounding them. And we try to lure them to the estate. And when they get there... that's when we close the gates. And that's when we burn the place down. Completely."

Silence followed. Aoife knew it didn't sound much of a plan. She knew it sounded reckless and ruthless. And she knew the moral ramifications of something like this.

But this wasn't the time for debating moral ramifications.

This was the time for action.

This group was a danger. A big danger.

And they needed to deal with the threat immediately.

"We'll have a few people stationed here, still. Waiting for Christopher's group to step inside. We lure them in. Trap them. Split them up. Scare them. And then we play them at their own game. We hunt them. Hunt them while they're disoriented."

"And what do we do with them?" Phil, one of the more cynical members of the group, muttered.

Aoife looked at him. And as cold as it made her feel, she knew there was only one answer. "We kill them. Every single one of them. Because they would not hesitate to do the same to us. They have never hesitated before."

She looked around at the group, and she felt an emptiness swelling inside when she said those words. She wondered if this was how Christopher felt when he commanded his people to capture people. To slaughter them. Because it was for food. Because it was "practical".

But then she pushed that thought away.

She couldn't start thinking about that right now.

She was nothing like he was.

This was different.

"I appreciate it's cold," Aoife said. "And I know it's not in our nature. But these people are a threat. I've... I've seen how they operate. I've seen what they do. How they act. And I know the only way we defeat them is through ruthlessness. Sheer ruthlessness. It's not what I... what I want. It's not what any of us should want. But it's what we need to do. To save our people. And to protect countless other people from facing the same fate."

Everyone was quiet. And she could only take that as a sign of reluctant agreement.

She gulped. A knot tightening, deep in the pit of her stomach.

Because she knew this wasn't going to be easy.

She knew it could very easily go wrong.

She just wanted more endorsement than blind following.

She wanted—

"She's right."

It was Cal who stepped forward. Who stood in front of the rest of the crowd. Right by Aoife's side now.

"We're peaceful people. But right now, there's a threat on our doorstep. And the longer we leave that threat alone... it's only gonna get bigger."

A few nods. Mutters of approval.

"So we stop the threat before it gets too big. And we owe it to our people. To our friends. They'd fight for us. So we'd sure as hell better fight for them."

More people clapped. More people cheered.

And in this moment of fear, this moment where it felt like standing on the brink, on the edge... Aoife felt her first sense of pride.

Of belonging.

But inside her, deep inside her, there was something else.

Something darker.

Vengeance.

Vengeance for what had happened to Max.

Visions of slicing Christopher's throat.

Was this what this was about?

No.

This was about their people.

This was about the future.

This was about—

"There's people out there!"

A shout.

A shout from the gates, up above. From the guard, Dina, standing up there, binoculars in hand. Eyes wide.

Aoife looked up there. Her skin turning cold. A hush fell over the rest of the community.

"What do you mean?" Aoife asked.

"There's—there's people out there. Coming this way."

Aoife's mouth went dry.

Time stood still, just for a second.

Then she climbed the ladder.

Grabbed Dina's binoculars.

Looked over the gate.

She didn't need the binoculars in the end.

She could see exactly what Dina was talking about.

And when she saw it, her stomach sank, and fear kicked in.

A group of people were emerging from the woods. Looked about thirty of them.

Only... no.

There were more than that.

She lifted her binoculars now and saw exactly what this was.

The people were holding other people on chains.

And those people on chains were naked.

They were prisoners.

People from this community.

From the estate.

"What do we do?" Dina said.

Aoife looked along the line, right at the edge of the woods.

Looked at them as they walked this way.

Saw the knives in the hands of those holding the chains.

Of Christopher's people.

And then she stopped.

She saw him.

Christopher.

Christopher leading the way.

A man in chains in front of him.

Knife to his throat.

And when she saw who it was, she almost dropped the binoculars to the ground.

It was Max.

## CHAPTER FORTY-SEVEN

Aoife saw Max in the distance and everything else around her disappeared.

He was on his knees. Wearing nothing but shorts. Chains around his body. And a knife to his throat. He looked a little bruised like he'd been roughed up a bit. Something that made Aoife feel a bolt of fury inside. Especially since it was so at odds with Christopher's so-called "peaceful" treatment of those in captivity.

But then, this entire scene looked at odds with everything Christopher had told her so far.

The mass of people lined up.

People from the estate.

People she recognised.

Chained up.

People wielding knives behind them.

It looked like the rules had changed.

She looked at Max. She thought he was dead. Thought he was gone.

And yet, here he was.

Alive.

Alive, but with the threat of his death looming over him, once again.

"What—what do we do?"

A voice beside her, cutting through the silence she'd been living in for the past God-knows-how-long. She looked to her side. Saw Dina, one of the guards on watch. She was always quite pasty, but she'd gone a new shade of pale now.

And Aoife could hear chattering down by the front gate. People all standing there, looking outside. The sound of terrified whispers.

The sound of their plan falling apart, right in an instant.

"What now?" someone else said.

And Aoife didn't know what to say. She didn't know what to suggest. She felt demoralised. Broken down. Because they'd spent so long this afternoon planning for exactly how they were going to fight Christopher and save their people.

And now, here they were. Right at their doorstep. All of their people in chains.

And Max, alive.

She looked back out over the gate. Christopher's people had stopped walking. They were all just standing there, all lining the woods. Like they were waiting for something to happen.

And Aoife could hear the crowd beneath her growing more impatient. Livening up. Shouting. Losing their composure. Losing their control.

"Aoife," Dina said. "What are we going to do?"

She looked out at those woods again. At the row of Christopher's people, all lined up before it. And at her own people, kneeling there, lives in danger.

Max, kneeling there, life in danger.

She saw them all, and deep down inside, she knew there was only one thing she could do.

"I have to go out there," Aoife said.

Dina frowned at her. "What?"

And after saying it, as scared as it made her... Aoife felt even more justified in what she'd said. Even more warranted. Even more *right*.

"I have to go out there," Aoife said. "And I have to speak with him. With Christopher."

"Aoife, I don't think they're gonna just let you walk up there and—"

"It's the only way," Aoife said.

Dina shook her head. Her blue eyes were wide. She looked like she wanted to stand up, wanted to argue. Then she just sighed and lowered her head.

"I don't like this," she said. "I don't like it one bit."

Aoife nodded. Lowered her head. Then she climbed down the ladder, right to the gate.

The estate people stood there and stared at her. Waiting for some kind of answer.

"I have to go out there," she said. "I have to speak with them somehow. It's the only way."

"But those bastards aren't gonna give you the time of day," Geoff said.

"I don't know what else to suggest. But I have to do this. I have to... I have to try and get to him, somehow. And I have to do it alone."

She turned around and went to walk towards the open gates, towards the woods, towards Christopher and his people, when she heard footsteps behind her.

"No."

She stopped.

Looked around.

It was Geoff, of all people.

Standing there. Red-faced. Fists clenched.

"What?" Aoife said.

"I said, no. You ain't doing this on your own."

"Geoff, I—"

"You said it yourself. Now don't go fucking going back on yourself. We're a community. And we stick together. You were right about that. Damned right about it. Whether you want to do this on your own or not... I ain't accepting that. None of us are accepting that. Unless you can give me one damned good reason why you're goin' out there on your own, I'm coming with you."

Aoife looked at Geoff, and as much as she hadn't liked the guy up to this point, she felt an overwhelming wave of emotion. He had her back. The whole community had her back. They were together, and they were going to stand by her side.

And she wanted to tell Geoff the truth. She didn't want to lead anybody towards death. She didn't want to lose anybody else and for that to be on her conscience.

But then she realised that it wasn't on her conscience at all.

They were choosing to stand beside her.

Because that's what community was about.

That's what *family* was about.

And that's what life itself was about.

She looked at Geoff. Then she looked at the rest of the people standing by them, all twenty of them.

She didn't know how this was going to go. Didn't know how it was going to turn out. She didn't know whether any of them were going to survive this.

She just knew one thing.

They were a community.

And they were in this together.

She took a deep breath.

"Well, in that case, come on then," she said. "We'd better go see what these psychopathic bastards want."

Some of the crowd clapped.

Some smiled.

But one thing was clear.

All of them were with her.

She turned around to the gate.

Looked outside, at Christopher's people in the distance, at the woods in the distance.

And then, together, they walked.

# CHAPTER FORTY-EIGHT

Aoife walked towards Christopher's people, the rest of the people from her community following closely behind.

But it really felt like there were only three people in this entire setup here, in a weird sort of way.

Her.

Christopher.

And Max.

She looked ahead. Kept her eyes on Christopher at all times. He was standing slightly to the front of the rest of his people. Max kneeling before him. Aoife hated to see Max like this. She'd seen him kneeling like this far too many times recently.

She knew how strong he was. She wanted him to get up. She wanted him to fight.

But she wasn't sure what exactly he could do about his situation. About his predicament.

He was down. He was chained. And he had a knife to his throat.

This was on her now.

This was on...

Then she heard them. The footsteps all around her. The nervous coughing. The voices.

And when she looked back, she realised she wasn't alone at all.

She was quite the opposite.

There were so many people gathered around her.

So many people here, standing with her.

So many people by her side.

She wasn't on her own.

She was far from on her own.

But then... Christopher wasn't on his own either.

She kept on walking until she was within about twenty feet of him. Then she stopped. She could see him clearly now. See right into his eyes.

She could see a newfound confidence there.

A newfound resolve.

But still that self-pitying look of a martyr.

Like he genuinely still thought what he was doing was right, in some way, somehow.

"Glad you could be here with us," he said.

"You didn't really leave us much choice."

Christopher smiled. "Look. I'm just saying. It's good that you haven't resorted to further violence. It's good that none of us have had to resort to further violence. And hopefully... that can be the way we move forward from here."

Aoife held her ground. Gritted her teeth. Beside her, Rex growled.

"What do you want?" she asked.

"It's pretty clear what we all want here, isn't it?"

"Don't speak in riddles. If there's one thing I half-respected about you, it's that you talk straight. Even if you speak complete and utter bullshit... you don't mince your words."

Christopher smirked. That cool composure looked like it was beginning to drop. His face looked clammy and red. "Aoife, we want one thing. What we captured. What was... what was ours."

"'What was yours'? What does that mean?"

"An opportunity," he said. "At first, I thought you were different. And I appreciated that. I respected that. Even despite all the horrors you faced. But... but then when you stood up against us... when you killed Cassandra... I thought I was wrong about you. I've gone through a lot of doubts. Now I'm wondering if maybe you're *exactly* the sort of person we want in our ranks after all. The sort of person we want to help lead us into a new generation. A new world."

Aoife stood her ground. Kept her gaze on Christopher. "What are you talking about?"

"You... you're strong. And that strength... that strength is something that doesn't end with you. It can be passed down through generations."

"I'm still not quite sure I'm following."

Christopher opened his mouth, then he closed it. "I just... I know this sounds crazy. And I know exactly what it sounds like. But I... Your genetics, Aoife. Your strength. Those are the... the kind of genetics we want passing on to the next generation. Because—because if we're to survive. If we're to move forward. We need strong people. Not just this generation, but the next generation, too. Do you see what I'm saying, now?"

Aoife felt sick. Actually tasted vomit right in her mouth. "Are you genuinely suggesting what I think you're suggesting?"

"I'm saying be pragmatic. To have an open mind. I know it's not exactly the most... palatable idea."

"You'd know a thing or two about what's palatable, wouldn't you?" Geoff shouted. "Fucking human-burgers."

Christopher glanced over at him, then looked away, sighing. Back at Aoife. "You have an opportunity, Aoife. And in return... in return, we back off your people. We back off your community. We let everyone go here but ten. Just ten. That's... that's not an easy thing for us to do. Especially when we're already low on... on resources. But it's a sacrifice we're willing to make. For the future of humanity."

Aoife felt herself turning cold. If there was one thing she could say of Christopher, it's that despite how batshit insane his ideas were, and his actions, they were always grounded in a weird sense of logic. Of pragmatism. Awful and horrible as they were.

But this... this was different.

He was speaking like a man with a God complex.

And she supposed it was inevitable, at the end of the day. A man in such a position of power.

It was always going to be like this.

"I don't know what's worse," she said. "That you're actually suggesting this at all. Or that you actually think, especially after everything, that I might consider accepting."

Christopher looked at her. Sighed, quite visibly. "Aoife, think about your people."

"I'm thinking about my fucking people," she said.

"But clearly not," Christopher said. "Because if... you've driven me to this. Remember that. But if you don't stand down. And if you don't cooperate. Then your people will fall, right here. And then the rest of your people will be ours. And you know what? You'll join us, whether you like it or not. But it'd be a whole lot easier for all of us if you could come quietly."

Aoife's heart raced. She saw the line of people, knives to their throats.

She looked into the eyes of Christopher's people. Saw them looking back at her. Wanted to find something there that she could connect with. That she could work with.

But there was nothing.

Nothing.

"So what's it going to be?" Christopher asked. "Are you going to join us? Join me? Or are you going to make this an unfortunate tragedy for everybody? Because I don't want that, Aoife. Nobody wants that."

Aoife looked at Max as he knelt there. Not saying a word. Just looking up at her with total confidence in his eyes. With total faith.

She looked at the rest of the people from the estate who had been kidnapped. Sam. Kathy. All of them lined up. All of them looking back at her, tears in their eyes. And the saddest thing was that no matter what happened here, the fate of some of these people was already sealed. All but ten.

There was no saving some of them. No matter what road she went down.

But no.

There had to be a way.

There just had to be another way.

"Aoife?" Christopher said. "What'll it be?"

She looked him right in the eye, and she knew she had no other choice.

She lowered her head, just for a moment.

Then, she looked back up at him.

"I'll... I'll join you," she said.

Christopher's face lit up. A glint to his eyes. "What?"

"I said I'll join you. But only if... only if *all* my people live. Every single one of them. Not ten. Not twenty. You let them go, and you leave them. All of them."

Silence. Silence cutting right through the woods. A few shouts of protestation from behind.

"That wasn't the deal," Christopher said.

"They're my terms," Aoife said. "You let them live. You give them a chance to walk. There'll be other people, just like you said. What's worth more to you? Me? Or these people? Because—because this is the only way I join you. What matters more to you?"

She saw his face turn. Saw it drop. Like the fantasy of Aoife's agreement had really got to him. Really brought him crashing back down to earth.

"Let them live and let them go, and I come with you. If you don't... it ends right here. For all of us."

She looked at Christopher.

She looked at Max.

She saw the tear roll down his cheek.

Saw the sparkle in his eye.

The smile on his face.

"I appreciate your nerve," Christopher said. "Really, I do. But that's not how we do things here. You're worth a lot. But not *that* much."

He looked at his people, and he nodded.

"Kill them all."

# CHAPTER FORTY-NINE

"No," a voice said.

Aoife wasn't sure where it came from. Not at first. It sounded like it came from one of her people. One of the ones on their knees, with the blade to their throat.

But it wasn't.

She looked down the line and saw exactly who it was that'd spoken up.

Who it was that'd shouted.

It was a man. Tall. Thin. Long, dark hair. He looked quite handsome. Probably about her age.

And unlike the rest of Christopher's people, who had knives to the throats of their prisoners, his knife was by his side.

He was shaking. Looked like he was crying. And shaking his head, side to side.

"This can't go on," he shouted. "Not like this. It just can't go on. This—this isn't us."

The rest of Christopher's people stared at him, still holding their knives to the throats of their prisoners.

Christopher looked over at him. His attention turned firmly from Aoife now.

"Dean?"

"This isn't us," the man—Dean—shouted. "I know we've done things. And I—I know none of us were proud of it. But we did it 'cause we thought it was the only way. The best way."

"Dean," Christopher said.

"But this—this isn't right. This bullshit about the next generation. And lining people up like this. Threatening to kill them all in cold blood. That... that isn't what we signed up for. That isn't *us*."

Aoife watched closely. She could see all of Christopher's people looking over at Dean, wide-eyed. Some of them had lowered their knives too. Others were still holding them, standing firm.

And she could see the looks on the faces of those on their knees, too. The hope. The optimism.

And she could hear the voices of the people standing by her all picking up. The mood shifting.

And she knew she had to act.

"He's right," she said.

Christopher looked around at her.

Everybody looked around at her.

Her heart raced. Her palms were sore from clenching her fists so tight. She couldn't get the fucking butterflies from her chest. And she really didn't want any more responsibility on her shoulders.

But she knew this was on her now.

It was all on her.

"I know how you've been living. I know the monstrosities you're all responsible for. And as much as I want to judge... as much as I'll never be able to look past that... I can't believe you're all just monsters. I can't believe you're all just killers. I can't... I can't believe you're all too far gone. I just can't."

"Aoife," Christopher said. Pulling Max close. Blade to his throat.

"I can't condone your actions. Nobody can. But can I believe you've done what you've done because you've been made to believe it's the only way to survive? That there's no other way? I... I can. I actually can.

"I'm not saying I can forgive. But I'm saying we've all done awful things in the name of survival. Things... things we aren't proud of. And we've got a long way to go. All of us. But if there's a semblance of emotion inside you telling you that this is wrong... listen to it. Listen to it like Dean here has listened to it. Because I don't care what Christopher says, and I don't care how fucking sorry he is. This is *wrong*. And it doesn't have to be this way. So put down your weapons. Put them down. Please."

Everyone stared at her. Wide eyes. She couldn't figure out those gazes. Couldn't figure out where they were all at, mentally. Whether she was getting close to winning them over.

But Christopher still had his blade to Max's throat.

His cheeks flushing.

His eyes watering.

"Aoife. This isn't the right way to—"

"She's right," another voice said.

Only it wasn't Dean this time.

It was a woman.

"Sadie?" Christopher said.

Sadie, who was short with long, dark hair, and very freckled skin, lowered her knife and stepped away from the man before her. "It's never felt right, what we do. But we've—we've done it 'cause we've been told it's the easy way. But this—this ain't how we do things. It can't be how we do things. I'm out."

Mutters amongst Christopher's people.

More people stepping aside.

Some still standing their ground.

But clearly enough mutiny to put a spanner in the works for Christopher.

To make him reconsider.

"Lower the knife, Christopher," Aoife said. "It's over."

Christopher's jaw tensed, and his eyes twitched. "So—so what are you going to do? Join these people? These people who are starving enough as it is? That really the solution, hmm?"

Dean shrugged. "I don't know what I'll do. But at least I'll know I wasn't a part of *this*."

And when he said that, it's like a lightning bolt of realisation went off in the heads of so many others there.

Because more people shook their heads.

Lowered their knives.

Stepped away.

And before Aoife knew it, it was just Christopher with the blade to Max's neck.

That's all she saw now.

"Put the knife down," Aoife said. "It's over."

She saw Christopher looking around, side to side.

Saw him looking over his shoulder.

Saw him pulling Max closer.

Like a cornered animal, knowing its days were numbered.

A dog, eager not to give up its prized toy.

"The knife, Christopher," Aoife said. "Drop the knife. This ends. This ends now."

He looked around at his own people again. And his face turned a new shade of pale, right in that instant.

The realisation.

The realisation that his empire had fallen.

That his dream had collapsed.

"Drop it," Aoife said, edging closer. "Drop it now."

And then he looked around at Aoife, and he half-smiled.

"I'm sorry," he said. "But I can't do that."

He pulled back the knife.

Then he swung it towards Max's neck.

# CHAPTER FIFTY

It all happened so fast.

Christopher pulled back the knife.

Swung it towards Max's neck.

A shout. From inside Aoife, instinctive, purely reactive.

Running towards him as quickly as she could.

Feeling like a mirror image of what happened with her and James six months ago.

She saw the blade getting closer to his neck.

Saw him arching away from it.

But the knife was getting closer.

And it was getting closer fast.

Too fast.

Faster than she could get to him.

She stretched out.

Tried to reach him.

Jumped in mid-air towards him.

And then something else happened, out of nowhere.

The man beside Christopher. Aoife didn't know his name.

But she saw him wrestle Max out of the way.

Push him to the ground.

And then she saw something else.

Christopher's knife.

It kept on going.

It kept...

Christopher's knife buried into Dean.

Right into his back.

Gasps. Shock on the faces of Christopher's people.

'Cause Christopher's blade was buried in the back of one of their own.

Dean lay there on top of Max, spluttering. Bleeding out. Blood trickling from his lips. He was a big guy, bearded. And he looked like he could take a punch or two.

But this knife.

This knife, right between his ribcage...

He lay there on top of Max. Staring up at Christopher. Trying to say something. Trying to speak. Blood oozing out, stopping him from speaking.

And Christopher just stood there. Eyes wide. Shaking. "I'm... I'm sorry. I'm..."

And then he looked around. Because his people were rushing over to Dean's side.

And then they were dragging him from on top of Max.

Surrounding him.

Trying to help him.

And as sad as Aoife felt for Dean, as grateful as she felt that he was the one who'd stood up for her, and the one who'd just saved Max's life... her eyes were only on one person.

Christopher.

He looked around at her. Wide-eyed. Like a rabbit in the headlights.

And then, just like that, he turned around, and he ran.

Aoife wasn't slowing for anyone anymore. She wasn't stopping for anyone. She'd see to Max soon. She knew he'd be okay because he was with their people.

He was with *her* people.

With her family now.

She raced through the woods, through the trees. She could see Christopher's figure up ahead, drifting in and out of the trees. Her heart raced. Her entire body felt tense. She wanted to catch the fucker. She wanted to catch the fucker and make him pay.

She didn't give a fuck about his apologies. She didn't give a fuck about any of it.

Because she'd seen his true colours at that moment right now.

Everyone had seen his true colours.

Without people around him, he was weak.

He was nothing.

Nobody was anything without the people around them.

She ran further into the woods. She could still see Christopher in the distance, but he was getting further away. He wasn't going anywhere. The snaky fucker could worm away all he wanted, but she wasn't letting him go.

She heard movement over her shoulder, behind her. Looked back. Saw people she knew running towards her. Christopher's people alongside them. And seeing them together, seeing them united... even despite all the horror and pain Christopher's people had caused, she knew that the only way people were going to move forward in this world was by pulling together.

She turned back ahead. She couldn't see Christopher anymore. The woods were growing darker. There was no sign of him anywhere.

She ran towards the thicker bunch of trees. Then out of them. There were no footprints. There was nothing at all.

"Where'd he go?" someone called.

Aoife went to keep on running when she saw movement behind the trees, down this slope.

She ran down there. The woods fell darker. The ground was muddy, an area untouched by the sun. There was a sudden coldness to the air. And in an instant, Aoife very quickly felt alone. Very alone.

She slid. Fell onto her back. Thick, slushy mud covered her hands, covered her legs.

Up ahead, a bird flapped away, making her jump.

She pushed herself up to her feet, tried to get her bearings again. She could hear people running behind her, but it sounded like they'd gone another way to her.

It was just her here.

It was just...

She saw something right up ahead.

Right on the ground before her.

A footprint.

A fresh footprint.

Only they stopped right here.

Then they moved over towards the trees, to her left.

Over towards...

She felt a hand around her mouth.

A sharp blade to her throat.

And as much as she tried to break free, as much as she tried to escape, she couldn't.

"Come on," Christopher said, holding her so tight she could barely breathe. "It's just you and me now."

# CHAPTER FIFTY-ONE

Aoife felt Christopher's hand tightening around her mouth, and she knew she was in deep, deep shit.

His palm gripped her face so tightly she could taste the sweat on his skin. His fingernails, slightly uncomfortably too long, pressed into her cheek so hard she felt like she might bleed. And the knife against her throat was a little too close for comfort.

Fuck. That was an understatement.

He had it right against her neck. Pushing so hard, it felt like her skin might slice at any moment. So tight it was making breathing even more difficult.

"Ssh," Christopher said, edging her forward. "We're going to go someplace quiet, you and me. We're going to wait for all this to blow over. And then we're going to have a serious chat about where we go from here."

She tried to kick back, but it was useless. Tried to shake free, but it was no use. His hand was blocking her mouth so much that she could see colours. She could barely breathe. And she wasn't sure how much longer she could stay conscious.

"Come on," Christopher said. "Nobody's coming for us. It's just us two now. Everyone else is a long way away. So why don't we just have a sit down and talk? A real talk about—about what's going to happen next."

Aoife tried to dig her feet into the dirt, tried to do anything she could to stop herself from being pushed along by this bastard.

But she couldn't get a hold on anything. Couldn't get any leverage. Her knees were weak, and her body didn't seem as strong as it could be, and she was struggling more and more to breathe.

The trees and the light before her pulsated with her heartbeat.

Christopher's whispers grew more and more muffled, more and more murky.

"Come on," he said. "Keep moving. Everything will be okay soon..."

She wasn't sure if she drifted off, if she passed out, but she must've done because the next thing she knew, she was sitting down. Propped up against something solid, something that felt like a tree.

Christopher stood opposite her.

No. He wasn't standing, exactly. He was crouched down. Crouched right before her.

Twirling a knife around in his bloodied hands.

Staring right at her.

"You're awake again. Good."

She tried to push forward, but she was tied back. Tied around her ribcage to this tree.

"Let me... let me go."

Christopher sighed. "That's not going to happen, Aoife. Not until we've spoken about everything that just happened. And everything that *has* to happen."

Rage built up inside Aoife. She pushed forward against the tie around her. "Nothing else is happening. You're finished, Christopher. Finished. Your people have seen you for what you are. How does that feel? That you've even become too much for your merry fucking band of cannibals."

Christopher never turned his eyes from Aoife, not once. "Maybe... maybe they were right. Maybe I did take things too far. But that's on all of us. All of us."

"Don't try and worm your way out of this one."

"What do you expect to happen now? Your people and my people just get along? That your people will really accept people like mine, knowing what we're responsible for? Knowing the things we've done? Take Dean. Sure, he might look a hero to you. But if I told you he butchered a whole family then went on to eat them, youngest to oldest, what would you say?"

Aoife tasted vomit in her mouth. And again, as much as she hated it, she had to admit Christopher had a point. These people of his were savages. They'd stooped to unforgivable lows.

And yet...

"I'm not saying we forgive," Aoife said. "I'm certainly not suggesting we become neighbours and friends. But... but all I'm saying is, at least they had something inside them that realised enough was enough. However deep inside and buried it might be, they still did the right thing when it came to it. But you... you still can't let it go. You would've killed Max. You killed one of your own. And then you ran. That shows me exactly what you are, Christopher. A cockroach."

Christopher shrugged. "Cockroaches are nature's great survivors. Maybe we could learn a thing or two from them."

Aoife shook her head. Coughed, the tie around her ribcage so tight. "You're insane."

"No," Christopher said. "And you know I'm not. And that's exactly what scares you about me, isn't it? I'm *not* crazy. I'm just a survivor. Like you."

"You're nothing like me."

"You've killed too," Christopher said. "You're just less comfortable hunting and consuming certain types of animals. And that's why I'll survive, and your people won't."

He stood up, then. Walked over towards Aoife. Knife in hand.

"We're not so different. And I'm not crazy. And that's what scares you the most out of everything..."

"So what now?" Aoife said. "Now that everyone's turned their back on you, what now?"

Christopher stopped. Looked like he was really contemplating what Aoife was saying. "They'll come back, in time. When they realise I wanted what was best for them. For all of us. And if they don't... well. I convinced them, didn't I?"

Aoife shook her head. "You're sick."

"Maybe so," Christopher said. "But when humanity's still standing in years to come, people might not know my name, but at least I'll rest easily knowing I did what I could to keep humanity alive."

"Ahh. Your 'next generation' plan. I forgot about that."

Christopher smiled. For the first time, he actually looked quite sinister.

"About that," he said. "Change of plan. I thought you were strong. I thought you were like me. But you're not."

He walked closer to Aoife. So close now, with that knife right in her eye line.

"You're not strong enough."

Another step closer.

"You're weak."

So close to her now, the knife was almost in touching distance.

"And you destroyed everything I built. For that, there's only one option."

He crouched right before her.

Pulled back his knife.

"You pay."

She held her breath, and for the first time, she smiled.

Because it dawned on her.

Where she was.

Exactly where she was.

Right where she'd hidden when she'd run away from the group in the dark that night.

The flashback.

The memory.

*"Hey, Dean? Stay away from those trees. You know the boss keeps his traps near places like that."*

"Hey, Christopher?" she said.

Christopher frowned. "What?"

"Stay away from the trees," she said. Clutching to her left, right to where she'd dodged the trap on that night. "I know how much you like to keep your traps near places like this."

Christopher frowned.

And then his eyes widened.

And before he could react, Aoife slammed the leg-hold trap right against his face.

She heard him scream. Heard him cry out.

Watched him tumble back, blood spilling from his cheeks.

Streaming down his face.

Watched as he writhed around in the mud, trying his best to break free of it.

As he dragged the metal teeth away from his face, pulling away his skin and his flesh in the process.

Watching as he kicked and screamed.

And as she sat there, against the tree, listening to Christopher's screams, she looked up at the sky. Looked as the sun began to peak through this dark, untouched area of the woods, blessing it with its light for the first time.

She looked up there, and even though she was alone, she smiled.

Even though she was alone, she...

That's when she heard them.

The voices.

The footsteps.

Voices and footsteps that she knew belonged to her people.

A tear rolled down her face, and she smiled.

She wasn't alone.

She never had been.

She smiled and cried and listened to Christopher's kicking and screaming as he tried to drag the teeth of the trap from his face, and she waited for her people to help her out of this.

She was not alone.

## CHAPTER FIFTY-TWO

Christopher opened his eyes and felt excruciating, splitting pain everywhere.

It was dark. Or rather... no. Somehow, even though it seemed dark, there was a strange haze to whatever room he was in. It certainly didn't feel like his home. It felt colder. Less comfortable. The floor he was on felt solid, and his back was upright.

He looked around, and he could faintly make out shifts in his visual field. Slight colours, but mostly greys.

He didn't know where he was. Or what was going on.

Only that he was in agony.

Total agony.

His head felt like it had been kicked a thousand times. And his face... oh God his face.

He had blurry memories of something bad happening. Of excruciating pain. But he couldn't place it. It was like his mind was trying to hide the truth of exactly what had happened from him. Like it was just too traumatic to go there.

He felt his stomach knotting. A bolt of hunger. A memory

that he had to get to work. That he had to get on with his day. That...

And then it hit him.

All at once, it hit him.

Aoife.

The stand-off between their people.

And then his own people turning on him, and Dean knocking Max out of the way, and Christopher's knife burying into him, and then dragging Aoife away and tying her up and...

It hit him then. The memory. The memory of that horrible sharp bolt of pain.

The teeth wrapping around his face, burying into his cheeks. Suffocating him, making him choke on his blood.

He reached up for his face, his vision really distorted, really muddled, and he knew what must've happened now. That trap. It must've clamped around his face and damaged his eyes.

But now where was he?

Where was this?

He reached out. Patted his hands against the cold, hard floor. It felt familiar, somehow. Like he'd been here before.

He patted and searched and desperately tried to find a clue as to where he was and how to get out of here when he felt something.

Something warm.

Something... like skin.

Feet?

Legs?

He tried to speak, but it was painful, difficult.

"Who's... who's there?"

Then the feet moved back.

He looked around. Tried to focus. Tried to see through this haze of grey.

And then he saw her.

Hard to make out properly. Looked blurry. Very blurry.

But there was no doubting it.

It was *her*.

"Aoife," he muttered.

"So you can see a little bit," Aoife said. Her voice echoing around whatever room this was. "Good."

He couldn't see her properly. Couldn't focus on anything at all for long.

But when she did drift into view, Christopher saw her staring right at him with a cold, hard stare.

"I'm glad you're awake," she said. "For a while, I wasn't sure if you were going to make it. But dying like that would've been far too easy an out for you."

She walked out of sight. Out of view. Christopher looked around. Tried to see her. Tried desperately to see where she'd gone.

"Please," he said. "I... I just did what I had to. We all did what we had to."

A laugh.

A laugh from behind him.

"See, you're showing your true colours now, aren't you?"

Footsteps to his right.

"You're showing exactly what you really are, now you're on your own. Now you've got nobody."

Footsteps behind him.

Then before him.

"You said you were a cockroach. Remember that? Well, we'll see about that."

He spun around even more when finally, he felt a cold, sharp thing that could only be a knife press against his throat.

Aoife stared down at him. Spinning, hard to focus on, but undoubtedly *there*.

"I could kill you right here," she said. "That would be the kindest thing to do. But you don't deserve the kindest outcome."

And then she did something he wasn't expecting.

She lowered the knife down.

Placed it in his hands.

And then, before he could get his bearings, she was gone.

"You're locked somewhere you're never going to escape. I've made sure of that. The trap, it really messed up your eyes, so I'm surprised you can see anything at all. But fortunately, you've still got your mouth, your tongue, most of your teeth. So you'll still be able to eat."

Christopher's heart did somersaults. Palpitations were always a problem when he was nervous. "What—what is this?"

"I *hate* to have to do this," Aoife said. "I'm really sorry." Voice laden with sarcasm. "But frankly, it's going to be very difficult feeding you. Keeping you alive. There's a portable stove over to your left. And there's a plate beside it. And a bowl, too. A nice, large bowl. I've even left some foil, too, so the flies don't get to your food too much."

"My... my food?"

"There's a knife in your hand, Christopher. And you've got a load of meat on your body. Plenty of meat on those thighs. In a few days, you'll begin to starve. And as you well know, the instinct to eat can be strong. Very, very strong. But how strong, Christopher? How strong?"

Christopher's stomach dropped. This couldn't be real. This had to be a nightmare.

"So go on. If you're hungry, why don't you tuck in? If you're so pragmatic, so serious about survival, cut away your flesh. Cook it. Eat it. You'll die eventually, of course. Probably very soon. But it's like you said. You're a cockroach, right?"

Christopher shook his head. Felt salty tears falling over the wounds on his face. "You—you wouldn't do this."

"That's where you're wrong," Aoife said. "I *am* doing this. And I'm going to come and visit you, every single day, to see where you're up to. I'll leave you water. I'll keep you alive. But you're not getting any food from me. None at all. So just how desperate are you to eat, Christopher? Just how desperate are you?"

Christopher shook his head. Tears streamed down his burning face now. "You're—you're a monster."

Aoife laughed. "Maybe so. But it was you who did this. You. Don't you forget that."

She looked into his eyes. He saw her, just for a moment, like staring at her through a fish-eye lens.

"Now come on," Aoife said. "Have a good think about how you're going to approach this. You're going to have a lot of thinking time, anyway."

A hand on his shoulder.

"But if you ask me... get that meat off those thighs of yours before you waste away. The more, the merrier, hmm?"

She patted him on his shoulder.

Then she disappeared from view.

"No," Christopher said. "No. Please. Aoife. Please!"

He heard banging. Shuffling around.

Then he heard something slamming.

"Aoife! Please!"

But as much as he shouted. And as much as he struggled around this dark, damp metal room... he knew he was alone now.

Alone with just a knife.

A stove.

And a plate.

He moved over to it. Crouched opposite it. Sat there, and he cried.

He thought of Mum. How much he'd just wanted to do her proud.

And the disgust he'd felt when she told him and the boys to eat her.

How wrong it all got.

How out of hand everything got.

His brothers.

Gingey, the cat...

And how after that point... he'd just gone with the easiest option of capturing humans because he was inept otherwise, and he was afraid.

And now it was gone.

All of it was gone.

He inhaled sharply.

Moved the knife around in his hand.

Hovered it over his right thigh.

*Get that meat off before you waste away...*

He pushed the knife against it.

Went to cut.

Heart racing.

Visions of the smell of his own flesh.

The taste of it.

And then the knowledge that he was going to die anyway.

He went to push down harder when he yanked the knife away.

Gritted his teeth.

Thought of Mum.

Thought of his brothers.

Thought of happier times.

"I'm sorry, Mum," he said. "I know... I know this isn't what you wanted for me. I know this isn't how you wanted me to turn out. But I tried. I... I tried."

He clenched his tearful eyes shut.

Pushed his knife down against the inside of his left arm. Hard.

Then, he cut.

He moved it over to the other wrist as blood pooled out. Sliced down deep, right into the flesh, right through the veins.

And as the hot blood oozed over his skin, the only warm thing in this room, he dragged himself over to the wall, and he sat there, upright, eyes closed, thinking of his mum. Thinking of his brothers. Thinking of better times.

"I'm sorry," he said. Crying. Smiling.

Images of being on a beach.

Images of being on a boat.

Laughter.

Happiness.

And then...

Images.

Images of the people he'd killed.

The people he'd eaten.

Images of them all staring back at him.

All surrounding him.

Darkness filling his mind.

"I'm sorry," he screamed, as his vision grew blurry.

As his ears began to ring.

As the taste of vomit filled his throat.

"I'm sorry!"

He saw the faces of the people he'd killed surrounding him.

And he saw Aoife at the front of them.

Holding the hand of his mother.

Smiling.

"I'm sorry," he said. "I'm..."

And then, as Aoife and his mother stood there, laughing, he drifted off into a painful, fearful darkness.

The last thing he felt?

Shame.

# CHAPTER FIFTY-THREE

Aoife stared at the bottle of gin in her hand.

She imagined the taste of it. The strong, burning sensation as she gulped it down. That slightly dizzy, light feeling as she got further and further into it. Quite delicious, in all truth. Definitely grown on her.

Then she smiled and put the bottle into the bin.

She wouldn't be needing it anymore.

She wouldn't be needing *any* booze anymore. Hadn't drunk for two weeks.

And she felt a hell of a lot better for it.

She got up. Walked over to her curtains. Opened them. Outside, she could see people on the streets already. Smiling. Going about their lives, happy. And nobody coughing, which made a goddamned difference, too.

The summer sun was bright. She could see kids playing. Hear laughter.

And it felt good. Seeing the community return to some semblance of normality, especially after everything they'd been through. Forty-one of them now. Nobody had died of COVID for ages. And everyone was relatively well-fed, especially after a few lucky hunts lately.

Well. Luck, and a bit of direction and assistance from her.

She heard panting. Turned around and saw Rex standing there, right beside his bowl.

"Oh, someone's hungry, are they?"

Rex rolled his ears back, wagged his tail. She went over to him, petted him. Laughed and smiled. And the overriding feeling she felt? One of gratitude. Gratitude for being here. And for having people around her.

Gratitude for being alive.

She thought back to that day two weeks ago. The day when everything came to a head. Snapping that trap around Christopher's face. Watching him writhe around and scream.

And for a moment, just for a moment, feeling a sense of total fear.

But it didn't last long. Because it wasn't long before Aoife's people—the people from the estate—arrived.

Before they joined her.

Before they helped her out of her ties and saved her.

She thought back to the time after that. To Christopher. To where she'd taken him. And to what happened...

And then the other memory.

She tried not to think about that memory.

That was for her and her only.

She watched as Rex chewed the meat in his bowl. There was a real healthy portion of it. They'd been in luck. Found an old warehouse in the middle of nowhere, packed to the brim with canned foods. Her discovery, too, which had only increased her popularity. Had a few good hunts, too. It seemed like their luck was really turning. The community was finding its feet again.

And most importantly, they were able to stay here. To stay home.

They weren't going anywhere just yet.

She sat there beside Rex, watching him eat, ruffling his fur. She was growing more grateful for these little moments lately. These moments of connection. She tried to make it her priority that no matter how brief the moment may be, she'd be fully present. Fully present for whatever happened. Fully present with whatever felt special.

She heard a knock on the door.

She stood. Didn't even feel a flicker of the hesitation she might once have felt.

Because there was nobody here she resisted anymore.

There was nobody here she pushed back against.

Because she let people in now.

She opened the door.

And when she saw who was standing there, she smiled.

"Hey," Aoife said.

Max smiled. "Morning."

"How you getting on?"

"Oh, you know," he said as he fussed Rex. "Getting by."

"Surgery coming along okay?" Aoife asked.

"Let me think. Doris came in with a bad foot; the worst problem I could find with it being that it reeked like mad. And Arthur's anal warts returned. So yeah. Quite the eventful morning."

"Gross," Aoife said. "As long as you keep those hands away from me, all's good."

Max laughed. "How about the supply runs?"

Aoife nodded. "Good. It's nice to be able to hunt again. Dad would've been proud."

"And the warehouse. You did well to find that. Right out of the way. But not a bad find at all."

A slightly sickly taste to Aoife's mouth.

Then, a smile.

"Well. We deserved a little bit of luck, didn't we?"

Max smiled. But the way he looked at her... it was as if he knew.

Like he knew the truth.

The full truth Aoife was hiding.

"Anyway," Max said. "I only dropped by to give you something."

"Buying me presents, are we?"

"It's nothing. Just a little... a little something. Slightly better than the last one I gave you."

Aoife frowned. "Go on. I hate surprises."

Max reached into his back pocket, face blushing a bit. And then he pulled something out. Something that fitted into his palm. Handed it to Aoife.

"What is it?" Aoife asked.

"What is it? Come on. You surely know by now."

"Oh," Aoife said, looking down at the little wooden object in her hand. "Another... another car, right?"

Max groaned. "A boat. It's a boat."

"Right," Aoife said. Trying to stifle her laughter. "A boat. I forgot that's what I'm supposed to say."

Max narrowed his eyes. "It means something, you know? Like, there's a meaning to it."

"Are you going to get all philosophical on me again?"

"I once told you that avoiding connection is avoiding living. Remember what you said to me?"

"I probably didn't take very kindly to it at the time."

Max smiled. "No. No, you didn't. But now you see it. I know you see it. I can see it in your eyes."

Aoife looked at the floor between them. "That's probably just the whites of my eyes. The drinking kept them pink for a while."

He smiled. And when he smiled, she felt that warmth inside again. That connection.

"I thought I'd lost you," she said. "And I thought the last damned conversation we were going to have outside of that hell-hole was the one in the woods. Where I said those things. About—"

"It's done now," Max said. Nodding. "We don't have to go there again."

She wanted to say sorry.

She wanted to hug him.

She wanted to tell him she loved him again, just like she'd told him when he'd almost died. Just like he'd told her.

But neither of them had gone there.

Neither of them had acknowledged it since.

And weirdly, it felt like it might never be acknowledged.

"You did the right thing, you know?"

"What with?'

"Taking Christopher's people to someplace new. I wasn't sure about the idea at first. But the more I think about it... the more I'm sure they deserved a second chance. Far, far away from here."

A knotting in her stomach.

The smell of burning.

The sound of screaming.

She gulped, and she smiled. "Did what we had to do. Like you said."

He looked at her. And the way he looked at her, for a little longer than she was comfortable, she wondered.

Did he know?

Did he know the truth and was just testing her?

"Anyway," he said, breaking the silence.

"Right."

"I'd better be off. Plenty more arse warts where those last ones came from."

"A delightful new pandemic."

He turned away. Still holding eye contact.

And she felt like this was the moment to tell him again about how she felt.

This was the chance.

"Max?"

He stopped. Looked back. "Yeah?"

Her heart raced. Just get it off your chest, you silly bitch. Just get it in the open.

Then she shook her head. "It doesn't matter."

He looked at her. Like he was giving her another chance to speak.

But in the end, he just half-smiled back and nodded. "Well. See you later."

"Yeah. See you."

She watched Max turn around and walk off into the light.

Off into this peaceful, safe haven of their own.

She stood there, Rex by her side.

Got a flash of the screams.

A flash of the smell of flesh.

And then a flash of the charred bodies and the silence that followed.

But at least she had her people.

At least she had her home.

She looked down at Rex.

Smiled.

"Come on, lad. Let's go to work."

She walked out of her house, closed her door, and stepped out into the light.

She saw Sam walking down the road, smile on his face. Kathy by his side. The two of them back to helping lead the group. The two of them saved from the clutches of Christopher.

The two of them saved like so many others.

Sam looked at Aoife and smiled. "How you doing?"

In the days before, Aoife would have nodded. Or even ignored them if she could get away with it.

But right now, Aoife smiled back at him. A genuine warm smile. "I'm good, Sam. I'm doing good."

And she saw the way he smiled back at her, the way Kathy smiled back at her, and she knew she wasn't alone anymore.

She wasn't afraid anymore.

This was her life now.

This was her family now.

This was her home.

And she'd do whatever the hell she had to in order to protect it.

She took a deep breath and swore she could still smell the stench of burning flesh...

# CHAPTER FIFTY-FOUR

***One week ago...***

Aoife stood outside the old delivery warehouse just off the motorway and ran through the plan in her head, again and again and again.

It was hot and humid. Aoife was sweating like mad. Could be nerves, too. Her heart was doing somersaults, which it always did when she was nervous about something. Kept on feeling like it was skipping a beat.

She was usually good at handling her nerves. A few deep breaths in, stimulating the vagus nerve, something she'd read online in the wake of her career collapse and life change.

But right now, she felt overwhelmed.

She wasn't sure about what she was going to do.

Wasn't sure it was right.

But deep down, she knew it was exactly what she had to do.

The warehouse she stood just outside was an old delivery unit. Really barren location. Industrial blocks and not a lot else, although they had tried to build a few student flats around here just before the power went out. She remembered coming here once when she'd missed a delivery for an iPhone. The bastard behind the counter wouldn't let her have the item unless she showed three forms of ID.

Three forms of ID? Who the fuck has three forms of ID?

A few months later, she read he'd been sacked for stealing. And the entire company went under because their business was rife with corruption.

There was some justice in the end.

She stood outside, looking in, watching. She'd thought this moment through so many times. It was two weeks since the confrontation with Christopher, two weeks since she'd clamped that trap on his face, then locked him away and left him with just a knife to get himself out.

She was disappointed how quickly he folded, really. Went in a day after locking him away and found him sitting in a pool of his own blood and shit with his wrists cut. She felt annoyed that he'd got the coward's way out. She wanted him to suffer. She wanted to *see* him suffer to the point of having to slice his own flesh away. Having to eat it.

But he was gone. That was the main thing. He was gone.

And now she just had to deal with the rest of his people.

She thought back to when she'd got back to the community. Most of Christopher's people had stood down. Surrendered. A few of them had fled, but the vast majority of them were on their knees. Repentant. Very repentant. Pleading for a second chance, fully aware of the wrongs they'd done.

And Aoife felt it. She really did feel it. Some of these people weren't *evil.* The more she lived in this world, the more she wondered if there was any such thing as evil at all.

But then she swallowed a bitter lump in her throat.

What she had to do was necessary.

In the two weeks since the events with Christopher, Aoife had found herself a job. She was one of the lead scouts and hunters. She was good at hunting, good at surviving, so it stood to reason that her skills were finally being put to use.

And she was happy about that. Happy that she was off the booze. Happy that she was making herself useful.

And happy that as scary as it felt, she was letting other people in.

Letting herself connect.

She heard the muttering inside. Heard people's voices picking up. And she knew it was time. The plan was simple. As much as Christopher's people had done awful, unforgivable things... they were repentant. They seemed genuinely sorry for their actions, willing to pay the price.

But the estate people had decided that they should be allowed to live. That their people were different to Christopher's. Even though they'd done awful things—fucking awful things—they'd shown genuine remorse. And they'd actually stood down. In some ways, without them, Christopher wouldn't have been defeated.

It was Aoife's job to take them out. To take them to their new home. To escort them away.

She thought back to the trip on the road. All of them behind her. All following, cuffed and blindfolded, but following. Three more people from the estate joining Aoife. Spirits seeming high. Things feeling... good, all things considered.

And then she'd told the other guys she was okay taking them on the last stretch.

She'd watched as Calvin, Helen, and Serge turned away.

Watched as it was left to just her to escort these people along to their new home.

Watched as they'd cooperated so, so well.

And now she could hear them.

Inside the warehouse.

The warehouse that she'd visited before.

She tasted a bitterness in her mouth. Wondered whether she could go ahead with this. Wondered whether it was the right thing to do.

But then... deep down, in her bones, she knew there was no other way.

She stepped out onto the balcony that overlooked the warehouse.

It was a huge, open space. Totally empty, but for a few rusty old delivery vans back from the old company who used to run this place.

And in the middle of the warehouse, she could see them.

She'd moved them into a circular section with steel fencing surrounding, right in the middle of the warehouse. They hadn't asked any questions. Hadn't asked a thing.

But they weren't getting out of there.

She looked down at that circle. At them all cramped in there, all looking around. Trying to break free of their blindfolds and their chains. Trying to see.

And then she looked down at the trail on the ground, leading towards them.

"Are you sure about this?"

A voice. Just behind her.

She looked around. Saw Geoff standing there.

He looked as sweaty as ever. She'd never expected to form any sort of alliance with Geoff. He was the last person she expected to bond with.

But he was someone who saw this situation the same way as she did.

Different to how the council saw it.

Different to how even Max saw it.

She looked into Geoff's beady little eyes, and then she did the only thing she could.

She nodded.

Geoff sighed. "You're probably right. Not like we can just let 'um go. Not after what they've done."

Aoife didn't say anything.

She just turned to that circle, down below.

To these people.

Men.

Women.

But no.

She couldn't see them like that.

She had to see them for exactly what they were.

Cannibals.

Monsters.

*But what does that make you?*

She heard that thought, loud and clear. And she saw herself standing here. Saw what she was about to do.

And she saw just how muddied the morals of this world were.

She saw them, and she heard Christopher's voice in her ears.

*"We're not so different. And I'm not crazy. And that's what scares you the most out of everything..."*

She heard those words echoing in her skull, and the thought came to her mind that maybe that's why she'd really been so savage towards Christopher. So ruthless towards him.

Because as much as she hated to admit it... she saw something of herself in him.

"Are you ready?" Geoff said.

Aoife took a deep breath.

Looked down at that circle beneath them.

Then at the matches in her hand.

That roadblock in front of her again.

Did she really want to do this?

Was this really the road she wanted to go down?

She looked down at those men. Those women.

And then she tried to see them not as men and women.

She saw them for all the horrible things they'd done.

She struck the matches.

Then she held them over the edge of the balcony, hovered them over, just for a second, wondering whether there was still a chance to turn back.

Then she dropped them.

The silence that followed was suffocating. Intense.

First, the spark of the flame.

Then the realisation in that circle.

The panic.

The shouting.

The pushing.

The screaming.

She dropped more matches.

Dropped them and watched as those lines of petrol surrounded that wooden circle.

The circle hut Christopher's people were crammed into.

Trapped inside.

Felt the flames getting hotter, even from here.

Heard the screaming growing animalistic.

Begging cries filling the air.

And the smell of burning.

Burning flesh.

She looked down at those figures on fire, and she felt tears welling in her eyes.

She'd done what she had to do.

These people didn't deserve a second chance.

They deserved to pay.

"Come on," Geoff said. "Let's get the fuck out of here."

Aoife looked right down into that circle.

At the flailing limbs.

At the panic and the horror.

And just before she stepped away from the balcony, just for a moment, she swore she saw someone staring up at her.

A woman.

A woman around her age.

Staring right up at her.

Then engulfed in flames.

Aoife stepped away.

Walked away from the burning.

Away from the warehouse.

The sound of the screams getting fainter but still following her.

Still haunting her.

She didn't say anything on the walk back. Neither did Geoff.

But when she saw her home in the distance, she smiled.

"Come on," Geoff said. "Let's get—"

"This never happened."

Geoff frowned. "Huh?"

"What we just did. It... it never happened. Okay?"

Geoff's eyes darted from side to side. Then, he nodded. "Trust me. I ain't exactly keen on this comin' out either. Now come on. Long day ahead."

Aoife watched Geoff walk past.

She looked over her shoulder into the woods.

Saw that cloud of smoke in the distance.

Heard the screams in her mind.

Smelled that stench of burning flesh.

And then she closed her eyes, took a deep breath, and let it all go.

Christopher's people weren't going to be a problem, ever again.

She turned back to her home.

And then she walked down the slope and into the sunlight.

* * *

**END OF BOOK 3**

Avenge the Darkness, the fourth book in the Survive the Darkness series, is now available.

If you want to be notified when Ryan Casey's next novel is released—and receive an exclusive post apocalyptic novel totally free—sign up for the author newsletter: ryancaseybooks.com/fanclub

Printed in Great Britain
by Amazon

74579242R00154